The Haunted Town

Demons In Elmdale

Ryan E. Hunter

Table Of Contents

PROLOGUE

She woke up with a shock, a screech spilling from her lips. Beside her, the book slid from her husband's fingers and landed with a quiet thud on the carpeted floor. "What happened? You ok?" He asked, caressing her shoulder. At the touch, she leaped up, alarmed. "Did..did you feel it, Tom?" She queried him in a raspy voice, gazing around the room. "Feel what?" "Something slithering...over....our body." She asked frantically, flinging the blanket off them as quickly as if it was on fire. "Martha, you ok?" Her spouse inquired, taking up the book and setting it on the bedside table. He switched his attention on his wife who was shivering and had her arms about herself. She glanced towards her closet as she heard someone chuckling. Of someone youthful. Like...

"MATTHEW!!! OUT OF THE CLOSET NOW!" She yelled, heading towards her closet and filled with wrath now. Matt's antics were beginning to wear on her nerves now. He had been pulling pranks on them for a couple of months now because he wanted to go back to the home they had left three months ago. From Chester to Elmdale, Matthew still hadn't gotten acclimated to it. "Oh Matt..." She disregarded her husband's mumbling behind her. He made no attempt to get off the bed and confront his son's uncouth conduct.

Furious, Martha threw open the closet doors. "What is it?" Her spouse questioned her in a 'what-now' voice when she gasped loudly. Matthew wasn't in there. No one was. She claimed that she had heard someone chuckling but there was no one in the closet.

"That's...." She mumbled but stopped when she sensed something in the closet or someone who wasn't Matthew just up the top shelf. With her heart racing frantically in her chest, she let her gaze drift upwards.

"Wh....." She gasped but the words die down on her lips. As she gazed inside the dark closet, something leaped down from the top shelf. Beyond horrified, Martha took a few faltering steps back. It was a lady. Kind of. She had delicate white skin and jet-black hair with ember eyes that blazed in the darkness of the closet. She had blood red lipstick on, making her lips shimmer in the lamp light from the bedside table. She was strangely lovely. She gazed at Martha exactly like a savage animal looked at its prey. When she licked her lips, Martha's stomach plummeted in dread and she attempted to scream. "Mar- " Her husband yelled her name but stopped as their bedroom door kicked open with considerable force. With chills going down her spine, she turned to gaze at the person standing in the doorway. He wasn't someone who was there to aid them but someone who looked just like the lady in her closet.

Shaking, Martha took faltering steps back towards her husband who was lying on the bed, stupefied. His gaze moved back and forth between the invaders. When the person at the doorway smiled at Martha, she shivered. "Already hungry, Quinlynn?" The gentleman intoned mutinously towards the lady from the closet. As though suddenly coming back into his senses, Martha's husband rose off the bed and pulled her alongside him. "Who are you and what are you doing here?" He asked forcefully but Martha could hear his voice shake. "It's 2 am in the morning, are you coming to rob us?" The person in the doorway chortled. The sound of his chuckling made Martha uneasy and afraid. His laughter was brutal and there was something about it that she could not figure out. "We are come to rob...." The lady, Quinlynn drooled out the words as she walked out of the closet and into the bedroom. "But we don't need your goods. We need something extra from you."

"Quinlynn, it is my time. Why are you here?" The person at the door grumbled and crossed his arms over his chest. When the lady shifted her attention towards him, Martha's husband lunged for his phone. He had scarcely picked it up when the lady moved. Within a blink of an eye, she had him trapped against the wall on Martha's left. Terrified, Martha closed her eyes. "You think you can call for aid without us knowing?" Quinlynn snickered at Tom. Martha heard her husband fight but she could not raise her eyes to see what Quinlynn was about to do to him. She tried to cry for aid but her voice failed her. "Please, take anything you want but leave us alone." Tom implored the lady. The person at the door laughed loudly. "I'm afraid Mr. Reid, we are famished and we need to eat something." "I'll take you to the fridge," Martha blurted out. Tom's face was expanding and swelled as Quinlynn applied additional pressure around his neck. "Please. I will offer you everything you desire." Quinlynn chuckled mirthlessly at Martha's comments.

"It is not the food in your refrigerator that we need. It's you....." She drooled out the word, pointing her forefinger towards Tom. Martha hurried to take her away from Tom. Taking a fistful of Quinlynn's jet-black hair, she tugged, forcing her to let out a scream which made Martha's blood run cold. Tom coughed and slumped against the wall as he battled to breathe. The man stayed standing in the doorway as if pleased by the scenario unfolding in front of his own eyes. Taking the grasp of Martha's hands in her hair, Quinlynn turned around. Martha shrieked as her hands twisted and she let go. "No one can hurt me and particularly not some poor human being like you." Quinlynn hissed, her keen fangs apparent in the low lighting of the bedroom. Vampire? It was all Martha could think. Letting out a small cry, Martha closed her eyes as she sank onto the floor. "Matt?" She questioned Quinlynn hoarsely, thinking of nothing except her kid. "Who is that?" Quinlynn said, narrowing her gaze down at Martha. So they don't know about Matt. He ought to be secure. She pondered and sucked in a big trembling breath.

"Open your eyes, Mrs. Reid, you need to see this." The stranger spoke barely in her ear, his cool breath sending chills down her spine. She simply shook her head vehemently. She kept her eyes closed tight as she heard Tom cry. It was a blood-boiling scream which made Martha shake on the floor. "Just as I thought. People from larger cities taste considerably better." Quinlynn exclaimed gleefully as Martha heard the sound of her licking her fingers. "Now we have to keep this lady in storage alongside the others. We are running out of place Quinlynn, cease heading for the new search." The man was speaking, his words slipping out slowly.

Swallowing, Martha opened her eyes. Quinlynn and the man were standing alongside Tom who was unconscious on the floor. "Tom??" Martha crept towards him, tears gathering in her eyes. Just what did the lady do to him? "Tom? Honey?" She touched Tom's cheeks but he did not move. She gasped when she discovered little holes around his temples. Crying, she attempted to shake him awake. With her hands trembling, she felt his pulse. When she couldn't feel anything, she pushed her ear to his nose. He wasn't breathing either. He was gone. Martha shouted, pushing the heels of her fists into her temple. She cried for rescue but no one arrived. Quinlynn and her partner laughed at her.

"WHO ARE YOU? WHAT HAVE YOU DONE TO MY HUSBAND?" She yelled at them. They observed her, amused before the man moved nearer her. "I will show you." He replied, extending his hand to grasp. With her tears flowing down her cheeks and rage and terror burning through her, she spits on it instead. The guy's pleasant grin faded in a moment and before she could even blink, he had her trapped against the wall. Martha could tell that he was enraged now and for some reason, he appeared even more menacing than Quinlynn. "Instead of showing you what we do, you should see it instead." He snarled, making Martha quiver out of dread. His eyes on her, he put his hands to her head. She wanted to kick the person or attempt to flee but she discovered that she was bound to the place. She could not even attempt to talk. With a wicked grin, the man closed his eyes. She felt hundreds of needles shoot into her temples. She shouted but no sound came out of her lips. That is when Martha felt, all the blood pouring up from all over her body. First, her legs gave out but she didn't fall. Then she lost the feeling in her arms. Her skull throbbed as though it'd burst open. The last thing she saw was the face of the man. Net of black veins on his light skin.

CHAPTER 1

I'll then get my own room, yay! From the other room, Simone snorted at her brother's giddy voice. "Sweetheart, yes. Also, you are free to design it in any way you choose. She was told by her mother. Simone sighed as she surveyed the empty space she was in. It seemed more open and roomy when the furniture was removed. Some of the dark purple paint was flaking off. To stop herself from sobbing, she tightened her jaw. She would miss this space.

Are you finished packing, honey? Her mother took a quick look around. Yes, I'm finished. She responded, letting her words flow carelessly. Simone moved her mother aside and went downstairs.

The vehicle had already been loaded with everything. As Simone went outside, she wrapped herself in an embrace to combat the chilly early November air. "I've heard Elmdale gets a lot of snow." Behind her, her brother was speaking to her parents. They shook their heads and fluffed his hair before making their way to the automobile. Simone turned back as she approached the automobile to take a look at the home she had grown up in. For as long as she had lived, it had been the house she remembered and loved. She was now leaving. Forever. As she peered over the terrace, she could feel the tears in her eyes burning. She recalled spending hours there in the spring painting. Then she turned to gaze at the plants and veggies in the little garden to the driveway's left. She recalled her grandma whistling as she worked to sow the seeds and dig the hole. It was everything being left behind by Simone.

Simone, let's go forward now. As she settled into the passenger seat, her mother made a call. "Yeah. Whatever." She muttered as she climbed into the vehicle. "Jayden, take a seat back." In response to her brother's head peeking out from between the front two seats, her father replied. Simone rolled her eyes and sat back as he yelled and laughed. She put on the headphones and pulled out her iPod. She closed her eyes while loud music played. Then they started traveling.

Because Simone was startled awake when she felt someone shake her arm, she must have drifted asleep. She moaned aloud as her head ached. "What?!" She yelled at her brother, who was eleven years old. He rolled his eyes without saying anything and pointed outdoors. It was pitch-black, with gorgeous violet and orange hues in the sky. There were dense woods on both sides of the road, and no one was in sight. Or, "Dad wants to know why the elderly guy attempted to stop the vehicle." Jayden said as he watched his father go near the elderly guy with interest. The vehicle must have continued moving since it was no longer visible. Simone also got out of the vehicle. Her father turned to look at her as he heard the door close. Stay in the vehicle, Simone. "I...I'm good," Simone, pay attention to your father. Her mother sternly warned her, but she disregarded her.

I have made efforts to prevent everyone from relocating here. With his fingers pointed towards the board behind him, the elderly man remarked. It was twisted over and corroded.

"Welcome to Elmdale," it said. Simone swallowed and turned to face the elderly guy, whose face was illuminated by the headlights of the automobile. He wore worn-out, outdated clothing and had a hunched back. She observed that he was slightly trembling. He had long, unruly gray-white hair that matched his beard in length. Simone had a hunch that this man could be residing among the surrounding, tall woods. "Why?" She heard her father make an ambiguous inquiry. He had come to a halt around five feet from the elderly guy. "Elmdale residents never see the outside world again. They will always be Elmdale's. The elderly guy responded in a gentle, dejected manner. Simone unintentionally bit her cheek. "Oh. Then I suppose it's ideal for us. Her father grinned and remarked before turning around.

"Sir, Elmdale is ruled by the shadows." Simone's father waved his hand without looking around as the elderly guy cried out behind him. The hair on Simone's arm stood up, and her heart stumbled. Definitely not a good beginning. When her mother gave her a critical look, she wanted to yell at her parents to turn around but she swallowed and climbed back into the vehicle. The elderly guy didn't move from where he was. Simone saw him making a cross with his eyes closed as the automobile drove by in front of him. She continued to gaze at him, but the approaching night's blackness engulfed him.

As they reached Elmdale, she continued repeating the old man's words to herself. It was a little village with just three thousand people living there, according to rumors. It was surrounded by dense forests and hills. At the end of street three was the home they had purchased. Simone saw that every home was pitch-black. There was no visible light anywhere. Just after eight o'clock in the evening. Only the street lights provided light for the street and the homes. It didn't appeal to Simone. Jayden was silent next to her. His eyes were sometimes wide open and occasionally squinted as he peered about. "Ok. I retract what I just stated. I don't like this location. Their father slammed his palm on the driving wheel in response to his announcement. "Pay close attention, each of you," I said. Where the truck was parked in front of a home, he started by slowing the automobile down. "This is the only location where we can live peacefully. No of how you feel about this place, you will need to comply. Now, it will be our planet. He exited the vehicle after saying these comments. Jayden sank back into his seat and muttered something that Simone could hear. "Remain in your automobile. I'll assist your father. Simone and Jayden were left alone by their mother after she stated and exited the vehicle.

Simone allowed herself to quietly observe her surroundings. The residences on the street have a uniform appearance. a little garden and a tiny driveway. To the front door, take two steps. Right of the entryway, a large window, and left, a garage. Their home in the city had been more compact. Simone was curious as to why her parents had purchased this one on the cheap. Where the homes stopped, there was a road followed by tall woods. Her heart leaped in her throat as she stared at them. From behind a tree trunk, someone was looking out at them. She could make out a pallid face against the shadowy background. Simone leaned forward in her seat while squinting. Yes, a face was there. She took a deep breath and exited the vehicle while keeping an eye on the face that was looking at her. It vanished as though it had caught her attention.

Despite her better judgment, she sprinted after. SIM, HEY!!! She ignored Jayden as he yelled at her. Her mind was telling her to turn back and halt, but she persisted. She quickly ascended the higher area and stopped when she got to the first line of trees. In the darkness. She ran out of steam. She took a deep breath and turned around. She reasoned that it had always been a foolish concept. Whoever it was would have vanished deep inside the forest of trees. She stopped as she heard the crunching of dry leaves and the breaking of twigs. "Who's.....there?" She yelled weakly, but there was no response. She retreated even farther as she made an effort to quiet her racing heart. The noises continued. "Show me," I said. Simone spun around and narrowed her vision to see in the shadows.

I'm not here to do you harm. said sadly in a shaky voice. It had a male voice. Simone moved away a little bit farther. Identify yourself. "It's irrelevant. You shouldn't have relocated to this town or that home. What...what are you saying? Simone gave herself a big embrace and massaged her arms. Although she could hear her own heart racing, she was unable to flee. The village is ruled by shadows. Nobody is secure. She made an effort to visit him but failed. He had expertly camouflaged himself in the darkness. "That home you just moved into? It's also not secure.

Simone braced herself by resting her hand on the large tree trunk in front of her as her legs trembled and her mouth was dry. Why doesn't it - "Simone!! Why in the world are you there? She was startled when her mother phoned. She was standing in the middle of the street, staring at Simone who was standing a short distance away. Her mother's face was hidden from her view. She started, "I'm." "Go." She overheard the man say as he made his way once again further into the jungle. "Come back right now!" With difficulty controlling her rage, her mother murmured, turning back to the home. As she approached the road, Simone halted a little distance from her mother. She was directing the employees to move more quickly as her hands were on her waist. When Simone slowly turned to look behind her, the road immediately came into focus. at her mother's grave's shade.

Simone's throat suddenly became dry, and she was unable to scream. Her mother's shadow was not it. It is impossible. She desperately glanced at her mother, who was wearing a baggy white button-down shirt, trousers, and shoes, while the shadow was donning high heels and a hat. Additionally, it was longer and stronger. It then whirled around to face her. Simone struggled to breathe as she stumbled back and collapsed on the street.

All through the night, Simone tossed and turned in bed. She couldn't get the shadow's picture out of her head. It was there every time she closed her eyes. Her mother had earlier sighed at her and assisted her in standing. Simone attempted to glance at her shadow once again, but everything was as it should be. Maybe I was dreaming? She gave it another consideration. She continued to observe everyone's shadows throughout the meal after that. She was too worn out and terrified to reply when Jayden made fun of her for being frightening for no apparent reason. Although her parents had made several promises, including a wonderful start, she had scarcely paid attention. She was still plagued by the old man's and the forester's warnings.

Simone awoke as her alarm went off. She sighed and rubbed her eyes. Her head was heavy. She was unaware of the time she fell asleep the night before. She opened the bedroom window's drapes and peered out into the peaceful street, in the home directly in front of her, curtains were being opened, and in the home to her left, an elderly guy was getting into his automobile. She grinned. So yes, people do reside here. She pondered. Everything seemed to be normal as the sun rose in the sky, but it wasn't. Something didn't seem right, according to Simone. What was it that she was missing? She was clueless.

Her mother forced her and Jayden downstairs into the living room after breakfast to assist her with unpacking. When her father went to the mayor's office, he was offered a new position that paid somewhat less than his former one. This location is deserted. Simone arranged the bowls in the kitchen cupboard while Jayden muttered something to his mother. Jay, not you as well. We're going to be content here since it's a nice location. Her mother sighed, which she heard. "I meant to say, just peek outside. No birds are present. When we're just close to a forest, there are no pets like cats or dogs. Simone was still.

What was lacking was that. the sound of birds chirping. There have never been any birds. Why would they stay in the city when their natural environment is nearby? Her mother grinned and moved her head in the direction of the tall woods next to their home. Simone remained silent while continuing to scan the area for shadows. She thought she caught a glimpse of something twice, but when she turned to look, nothing was there. Her father came home at about seven o'clock in the evening.

Dear, how was your day? As she took his bag and coat, her mother questioned him. "Tiring. The town seems tranquil despite the excessive labor at the workplace. We'll be content here, I'm sure. At the table, Simone suppressed the impulse to roll her eyes. While she and her brother were watching television, she was listening in on her parents' chat. "I'm happy," Mother responded. Simone tilted her head to see as they up the stairs to their bedroom. She let go of the popcorn as her eyes became wide, Shadows. With their shadows, two of them were following her parents. "Jayden." As she pushed him with her elbow, she said. "Look at your parents." When he saw her, her brother screwed his face and turned to see. "I've known them my whole life. What has changed? He loudly enquired. She clenched her teeth and turned to gaze once again. Although there were no longer any shadows, her parents were still laughing at something up on the stairs. Had she had a new dream? She questioned.

Simone retrieved her camera that evening and sat on the window seat. She concentrated on the road outside. The curtains were drawn, the lights were turned out, and people were slipping into their homes. Everything soon fell into complete darkness. The street lights' dull orange light bulbs provided the sole illumination. "I have no clue what I'm doing," you say. She moaned and put her phone on quietly. She watched and waited for almost an hour without seeing or hearing anything. She fell asleep. She moaned and pushed her eyes to open so she could take one final glimpse outdoors as her head struck the window sill.

She would never forget what she had seen. The roadway was completely obscured by shadows. Simone let out a cry as terror made her skin tingle. What on earth was she observing? In the hopes that they would be gone and that it was just another illusion, she clenched her eyes shut. Slowly, with her heart thumping in her chest, she opened them. No, that wasn't a dream. There were shadows all across the roadway. They were tugging at one another on the streets and scaling the homes and streetlights. When Simone's legs gave out under her, she stumbled back from the window and fell with a bang on the bedroom floor. I uttered a noise. The realization horrified her. Sure enough, she saw hands on the glass of her window. She hurriedly laid down on the ground and pretended to be sleeping before the shadow could see her. She was certain that the shadow could hear her heart beating in her chest. She mentally tallied up to fifty before opening her eyes. Like it had been, it was pitch black. Nowhere could be seen a shadow. She sighed with relief and stood up, moving back toward the window as gently as she could.

Although the shadows were still there on the street, they were not as frantic as before. Simone heard the sound before she could ask why. The heels' clicking sounds may be heard as they move. The shadows began to vanish into the night, and those that were still on the path split up like waves for the approaching figure. Clicking, clicking, clicking, clicking She was a female. Simone gulped. She was not a shadow, and it was obvious that she was a threat to them. Right in front of her house, the woman came to a stop. Her heavy, black hair covered her face, and she had her back to the light. She swung around to face the entrance. Simone huddled behind the curtain while holding her breath while continuing to search. She had a pale complexion, vivid red lipstick, and bright red lips. When the woman turned her head to look out the window, she only saw that. Where Simone was standing.

CHAPTER 2

"Hey SIMONE!!" Her brother yelled, waking her awake. She woke up in shock. When Jayden ripped open her bedroom door, she yelled, leading Jayden to scream in retaliation. "Why the heck are you screaming?" He yelled at her. "Why the heck did you?" She responded. "I yelled because you screamed!" Jayden was saying, his cheeks crimson. Simone released an audible breath, her fingers pressed to her chest. "What is so crucial early in the morning?" "You've received a letter. No name, no address simply 'For Simone'." Jayden stated, adding air quotes towards the end. "Your name isn't even spelled properly."

Scrunching her face, she reached out for the envelope in Jayden's palm. It was yellow with age and harsh to the touch. "So.....who is it from?" Jayden replied, hopping up on her bed and pressing on her shoulder. She shook him off as she opened the letter. It only held a square piece of paper. And just two words:

' Remember '-' M'

"What the Hell is this?" Jayden said, giggling. Simone was perplexed. Who had sent her this and remember what? "Simone, Jayden. Downstairs now! You have to go to school today."

Their mum walked through the door and peered at them, her hands braced on each side of the door frame. "What is it?" She asked them. Jayden was still giggling as he got off the bed. "Simone's got a fan." He grinned as he leaped out in the corridor from beneath his mother's arm. "Sim, hon. Are you ok? When did you go to sleep last night?" Her mother enquired, making her way into her daughter's room, and flung open her closet. Shaking her head, Simone tossed the envelope and the message into her drawer. "I don't recall." She murmured. And she honestly didn't recall a thing about last night. Had she been so exhausted that she had gone to bed without even writing in her journal or putting out her clothes for school? Her mind was blank. Now, this was at first, Simone thought sulkily.

On the first day of their school, their father had dropped them there but beginning the following day they were to go by themselves. A vehicle was meant to arrive and pick up Jayden while Simone had to pedal her bike to her school which was only two blocks over. She hated her bike. It was pink and she had obtained it as a birthday gift from her parents on her fourteenth birthday. It was nearly two and a half years ago.

"Remember, strive to be pleasant, and make friends." Her mother continued and Simone grumbled loud enough to show her how miserable she was anyhow. She missed her former schools and her pals. "Hon, you have to attempt to fit in else you'll be an outsider forever. The first impression lasts a lifetime." Her father commanded as he drove his automobile just outside the school gates. Shouldering her virtually empty purse, she went out. Almost quickly she sensed that every eye was on her. From the females standing by a beautiful new red automobile to the lads gathering by the wall and smoking, everyone was staring at her. "Brilliant. Too much for remaining low." Simone grumbled and made her way toward the gates. Her face down.

"Hey, new gal!" A girl called to her. "Have fun, honey." Her mother yelled unhelpfully from behind her as they drove off. "Hey." Escaping was worthless and she didn't want to stand out doing it. The girl who had yelled out to her was one of the girls standing near the red automobile. She had jet black hair and a fair complexion. Her dark blue shirt and leggings were great on her. She was lovely. Eerily gorgeous. "What's your name?" She inquired, lifting her hand to meet Simone. "Uhh... Simone." Simone stammered before meeting the girl's hand. "Uhh...Simone, welcome to Elm High. I'm Brianna Hoskin." She remarked, copying Simone's introduction. Almost immediately, Simone understood that she did not like this female. "Thank you. Nice to meet you too." She remarked, continuing towards the gates. To her dismay, Brianna and her pals followed her.

"Hey, Bri! Stop pestering the new girl." A man screamed from behind them prompting the others to chuckle. "Shut up Nathan!!" Brianna yelled back making her companions chuckle. Typical teens...Simone thought. I detest it. I loathe it here! Simone thought fiercely as she went over her timetable. She shared three of her lectures out of seven with Brianna and her mates who opted to tag with Simone for the remainder of the day including lunchtime in a tiny cozy café. "Stay with us, you'd never be an outsider." Brianna was saying, chewing at her beef burger. How could she consume that much? "And you'd be popular and in the limelight." Her buddy, Jenna remarked with a wink. "And you'd get to hang around with guys too," Vanessa remarked coyly. Simone fought the impulse to beat all three of them with her fork.

The rest of Simone's day went in a whirl as she struggled to understand the ideas that were being conveyed. She had transferred amid the semester and it was going to be terrible for her to catch up. At the time, Simone was delighted to find out that Brianna and her companions were nowhere to be seen. They were probably in the cheerleading practice as they had told her they'd be. Glad, she swiftly made her way to her locker only to discover someone waiting for her. It was one of the guys who had been outside the gates in the morning.

"Can I help you?" Simone asked, appearing to be unconcerned and annoyed. "Nah, I don't need your aid." The man laughed. "I simply wanted to welcome you to Elm High." "Thank you?" She replied, scrunching her lips to one side of her face. "So how was your day?" He questioned her, flashing his dimples at her as he moved aside to allow her to reach her locker. "You care because?" "As a senior at this school and someone who is student body president, it is my responsibility to predict any troubles that may befall the incoming transfers." He explained, leading Simone to snort loudly in response as she struggled not to giggle at the usage of his words. "I had a lovely day, thank you." She flashed a false grin in his direction before walking away. Thankfully, he did not follow her.

It was dusk yet her home and the street was dark. Her mother worked in the kitchen while Simone and Jayden lay out the dishes on the table for supper. Simone watched her mother work. She seemed joyful and she was humming. Something she hadn't heard in more than two years or so. As she observed her mother, her gaze moved to her shadow. It was dancing. The shadow of her mother was dancing while her mother wasn't. Simone's eyes widen as she attempted not to yell in terror.

It brought back the memories from the night they had transformed. She had believed that it was some type of delusion but it wasn't like it wasn't just the night before when her parents were heading up the stairs. "You seem pallid," Jayden muttered unhelpfully, making Simone jump in terror. "What?" She croaked out. "Yeah, certainly scared since we've moved here." Her sibling commented and went back to toying with his fork and spoon. Simone wanted to urge him towards the shadow of their mother but she knew better. As she gazed in terror, two more shadows formed alongside her mother's.

They were tugging at each other as though they were fighting. "Simone?" She scarcely heard her mother. "Simone????" Her mother called out to her again. Then the shadows turned. To stare directly at her. "Hon, what is it? You're pallid." Shadows were coming towards her. Slithering from over the surfaces of the chairs and then the table. When they were barely a foot away from her, Simone shouted.

"Simone, honey are you up?" She heard her mother's anxious voice and clenched her eyes a little before opening them up. She was on her bed and three faces were leaned over hers. "What the hell?" She muttered as she gazed at them. "You yelled and then you fainted." "Nathan hauled you here upstairs, I had no clue what to do." "Why did you shout anyway?"

Everyone asked the questions one after the other but she was too surprised by the appearance of the lad from her locker to recognize anything else. What was he doing in her residence and in her bedroom? Consciously, she dragged her blanket to her neck. Only her face was visible and she was still staring at Nathan, her eyes narrowed. "She is bashful." She heard her brother speak mischievously. "I'm sorry Simone. I was just going by your home when I heard the scream. I didn't realize it was your home but I raced in anyhow to see whether everything was good." Nathan said shyly. "Honey, why did you faint? Did you notice something?" Her mother enquired, sitting down beside her. Did I see something? Simone pondered but she could not recollect. "I don't know. Where was I? I don't even remember yelling." She murmured, attempting to recollect the last few hours of her day but she could not. There was nothing. Her mind was blank.

"You sure?" Her mother questioned, her brow wrinkled with anxiety. "Yeah. I am. Where was I and what was I doing?" "Oh my GOD!! She doesn't remember! Are you suffering from amnesia or something?" Jayden inquired in a terrified tone with his eyes wide and mouth hanging open. Simone chewed her bottom lip as she gazed from one face to another. "I discovered you in the kitchen. You were fallen on the floor and your mother was attempting to rouse you up." Nathan replied, bewildered as he watched her. "Thanks for your assistance, sweetie. Jayden will show you to the door." Her mother replied to Nathan, faking a grin his way. Thank God, her mother remembered that there was a male in her daughter's bedroom. Uninvited one at that. As Nathan followed Jayden out of the room, he paused at the entrance to offer Simone an apologetic grin. She only nodded absently, her mind still attempting to absorb what had occurred to her.

Later that evening, Simone sat down at her desk and pulled out her daily notebook. The last entry was three days ago. Never previously Simone had missed more than a day or two of entry but this time, she had skipped three days in a row. Sighing, she put her head in her hands. She hated this place and everything about it. Nothing made sense and her mind were blank. It was exactly how it had been the night before. Feeling powerless and frustrated, Simone wrote down about her evening.

A week went without any incident. After her fainting incident, Nathan had taken it upon himself to escort her to every class. She disliked it and had urged him to stop doing it but he had shrugged and had behaved as if it was nothing. It should have been nothing yet it was. She could feel everyone's eyes on her. Simone frequently spotted Brianna and her pals observing her. She could not interpret their reactions but she knew that they did not enjoy Nathan's focus on her. When questioned why he was doing it, he had simply responded that since she was a new female and someone he wanted to know better. Simone had glared and left him in the corridor as she had bolted into the girls' restroom.

She still felt that she had hallucinated the shadows of her parents and from the night they had moved into Elmdale. It was on Wednesday when she got another letter. A note which read:

They're onto you.

Simone still didn't know who it was. She had retained the last one and that is where she stored this as well. Two days later, she found a strange entry in her daily diary. One she couldn't remember writing although it was dated the previous night.

I can't sleep, she'd wrote. I am sitting down at the window and staring out at the dark trees. A cool breeze is blowing. Winter is coming. My neighbors are awfully punctual. At precisely 9 PM, they are turning out their lights and draw the curtains. I should turn off my bedroom light too. I turned it off. The only light is coming from the street lighting outside. It's a gorgeous night. Now glancing at the road, I'm confident that I'd hallucinated the shadow there. I must truly detest this place but not at night. It's lovely. I want to... SHADOWS! HUNDREDS OF THEM. ON THE STREET. A WOMAN...

That is where the entry was concluded. She had penned the final lines quickly. She could tell. Just what had she seen? Why the heck she couldn't remember? She decided to stay up this night as well. This time with a camera.

Come morning, her head felt heavy and she was sneezing. Her muscles hurt as if she had run miles the night before which she didn't recollect. As usual. When her mother arrived to wake her up, noticing her condition she informed her that she'd be phoning her school for sick leave. Simone was thankful to her. When she was gone, she slipped back to sleep.

Hours later, her mother awakened her up for breakfast. It was 11 AM. "I need you to take some medication, bathe and eat. Staying in bed won't help you get well." She endorsed. Simon wanted nothing but to remain in bed for her head felt like a weight on her shoulders but her mother only departed after Simon had begun bathing.

After breakfast, she sat puzzling about weird notes in her daily journal. She noticed that she had written about the shadows once again and had written that she had captured last night's happenings but when she checked her camera, it was empty. Confused, Simone sat down on her bed and re-read the entries. It couldn't have been a joke because she recognized her handwriting. It was then that her mother peered into her chamber. "You have a guest." She said with a covert grin. Simone frowned. "Who is it?" "See for yourself." Her mother giggled, opening the door wide for no one other than Nathan. Simon frowned out loud. "Wow. Why do I feel like you didn't want anybody to visit you? Let alone me." He smiled from ear to ear as he made his way towards the chair. "Keep the door open youngsters." Her mother said and left. "I'm not suffering from illness or dying that you had to visit me and forsake your studies in doing so," Simone stated in a caustic tone. When Nathan flinched, she regretted it a little. He was looking out for her and he had been her only friend for the two weeks she had been here.

"I simply want to be your friend Simone. To know you better." "Is it because I'm the new girl?" She asked respectfully this time. "Yeah, is part of it." He said, scrunching up his nose. At that moment Simone understood that he was cute. "And the other part?" "Well, you're attractive and not like other ladies your age in this town." He muttered, rubbing the back of his head uncomfortably. Simone laughed out loud. "Guess not many girls talk to you the way I do." She smirked at him. "You've seen them. They very much want to worship the earth I walk on. It makes me feel uncomfortable." He grinned and then gestured towards her journal which she still held in her hand.

"What's that?" "My everyday journal." "Have you written about me in there?" He asked sheepishly, making Simone roll her eyes. Ok, he was cute but annoying. "As if. I write about the stuff that bothers me. Not the details of every minute of every day." She replied, putting it aside. Nathan continued glancing at the journal, a faint grin on his lips. Simone wanted to ask what was he thinking that was making him grin when Brianna barged into her room followed by Vanessa and Jenna.

Simone's eyes widen in amazement as Nathan's glared at Brianna. "Hey, darling. Learned that you became ill." Brianna murmured, ignoring Nathan gazing holes into her. "And you are here because....?" "Of course, we wanted to check up on you. Here, we brought you something." She clapped eagerly and dragged Vanessa forward. She was a girl with elegant light brown hair and little eyes. Simone wondered whether she was Asian. "We didn't sure which one was your favorite so we ordered Brianna's favorite instead. Hope you'd enjoy it." She added with a wink as she handed a package to Simone. Mumbling a thank you, she opened it up. It was a cake. Plain chocolate cake with 'GWS' inscribed on top of it. Simone disliked chocolate so she had to make a grin for Brianna who embraced her. "It was so dull without you today," Jenna remarked as the girls lay down on her bed around her. "I don't recall putting up a comedy performance or whatever in the two weeks I've attended Elm High," Simon murmured softly, making Nathan laugh so hard that Brianna flashed him a glare. "No, darling it's not. You are new in town. The last new person arrived here three years ago so you are unique and having you around is unusual. Refreshing." She said with a wink. Simone lifted her eyebrow heavenward.

"Anyway, let Simone rest today. She needs it." Nathan responded, rising and shouldering his bag pack. Brianne rolled her eyes at him but said nothing. One by one the girls hugged her farewell and were gone. The room felt warmer all of a sudden. Just then Jayden wandered in, still in his school uniform. He waved another envelope at Simone to spring from the bed in hurry to read it. "I guess you've gained an admirer. I truly love the traditional manner of delivering the mails." Jayden winked at her coyly. Simone slammed his head and shoved him out of the door.

'Stay away from them' -

That was all the note read.

CHAPTER 3

Simone attempted to recollect anything which she had to complete yesterday night but could not recall once again. This was driving her mad. Never once before she had forgotten anything. Was she sick? Or was it anything due to this town? She picked out her daily journal from her closet but to her dismay, the pages were gone. They were carefully pulled out of the journal. The missing pages resulted in a heated confrontation with Jayden which concluded with him weeping. He continued by saying that he did not know that she had been keeping her journal in the closet. Deep down Simon believed him but if it hadn't been him then who had pulled out the pages? This is very wonderful!! She pondered, pacing her bedroom. I'm going mad!!

"SIMONE...." Her mother summoned her down the stairs. Biting her bottom lip, she made her way down. It was Saturday and her mother had asked two of their neighbors around for the supper. She was bringing out her beautiful china from the cabinets. One they were not permitted to use at home. "What is it?" "I want you to drop by your dad's workplace and give him this lunch box." She had, moving her head towards the package on the table. "And after that I want you to purchase some goods from the shop. The list of the goods appears beside the box." "Anything else?" Simone questioned, eying the things on the list. So her mother was going to host a feast. "No. And be back as soon as you are done. I want you to assist me in fixing supper." "Whatever," Simone murmured, her attention firmly on the missing pages of her journal.

Outside the mayor's office, Simon parked her bicycle in the bicycle rack and proceeded towards the stairs of the building. A lady attracted her attention. A lady clothed in red and black. Her back was facing her so she could not see her face. Simone halted in her steps and observed her. Something was odd with her, something Simone could not pick clearly. She had straight black hair down to her waist and was clothed in a red coat and pencil skirt. Her shirt wasn't visible. An elderly guy dressed in a suit caught her watching. He nodded at the lady and switched his focus towards Simone. "Can I assist you, child?" He questioned, evidently displeased by her gawking. The lady went immediately, without turning to look at Simone. Click, clack, click, clack.....

The sound of her red heels sent goosebumps down Simone's spine but she could not explain why. "Young woman, I asked you what are you doing in front of the Mayor's office?" The elderly guy inquired again when she persisted in gawking at the lady departing. "I.....I...I'd simply come to bring this lunch box to my father." She remarked, suppressing the impulse to peek at the lady who was at the building doors by now. "And what is the name of your father?" "Ian Dawson," Simone remarked, faking a smile at the elderly guy who was glaring at her with sour disgust. "Ah, the new man. Hand the package over to me, I will deliver it to him." "No, it's alright. I'll deliver it personally." Simone said hurriedly. He lifted his eyebrow heavenward at her. Without any further remark, he lifted his hand for the box. Twisting her jaw and tightening her free hand into a fist, Simone gave over the package and headed towards the bicycle rack without a second look. What was wrong with the folks here? She pondered as she got on her bike.

The ride to the shop took even less time. The town was too dang little. As predicted, the shop was tiny and the things were packed on the racks which were nearly reaching the ceiling. Simone caught herself when she fell over a crate just inside the main entrance. "Welcome." She lifted her head to look at the guy behind the counter. His voice sounded familiar. "Can't say that I feel welcomed. I nearly tripped." Simone fired back without thinking. The man opened his lips to say something but then closed them. He feigned a grin and with a little nod, he went back to his task. "Great. These guys certainly need lessons on appropriate conduct." She groaned gently as she took a shopping vehicle. As the shopping cart got caught here and there as she shopped, she continued thinking about the lady she had seen outside the mayor's office and also about the gentleman at the counter. When she approached the counter, she observed his expression as he surveyed the things in her cart. He looked like someone about her age but was tall around six feet. His wavy brown locks were disheveled beneath his blue hat which had the store's emblem on it. He donned a similar shirt which hung loosely on his small frame. As if feeling her gazing, he glanced up at her. "Is there anything wrong?" He inquired coolly. "We've....we've met before, haven't we?" She questioned him, studying his expression intently. He stilled but made no effort to meet her stare. "We've chatted previously and....." She paused. He was the lad from the woods. The one who had warned her the night they had relocated to Elmdale. "Not here." He muttered as he gave her the receipt. "Meet me where we met at five. Make sure there is no one observing." "But...." "I hope that you liked shopping at Elm Store. Welcome to Elmdale." He remarked in a professional tone, cutting her comments.

Simone wanted to remain and make him speak but after one glimpse at his expression, she decided that she'd rather meet him in the woods. "Thank you." She smiled at him and departed. Just outside the shop, she ran into Brianna's co. "Oh my, what are you doing here?" Vanessa inquired, dressed in all black. It felt unusual to see them without Brianna. "Just shoppin'," Simone said, heading towards her bike. "Cute bike you've got there." She rolled her eyes at Vanessa without turning back to look at them. When she got onto the bike and looked at the girls, she saw Jenna looking at her strangely. The other one had already disappeared into the store. Simone lifted her eyebrow questioningly at her. Jenna simply gave her a horrible grin. Full of hate and danger. Unconsciously, Simone gasped and looked away. She could feel Jenna's eyes on her all the way until when she rounded the corner. What was wrong with the girl?

She was in a fog as she assisted her mother. She kept thinking about the man in the supermarket. At approximately 5:15 the visitors rolled in. Two of them were ladies in their forties while one of them was like Simone's mum. After welcoming them, she raced out of the home. It was silent. Just like every other evening in Elmdale. Sunlight just highlighted the top of the trees. After glancing along the three roads beside her home, she raced into the forest. She didn't stop. She continued running, feeling out of breath as the earth climbed higher and higher as she rushed more within the forest. "I worried you wouldn't arrive." She came to a standstill at the voice. She was breathing heavily and her legs hurt. "Guests." She gasped and turned to face the man from the shop.

He wore a casual brown t-shirt over blue pants. His wavy curls were still unkempt. He had his arms wrapped across his chest as he rested against the tree trunk. "They didn't notice you leaving, did they?" He inquired and she merely shook her head. "Why did you warn me the day I changed in this town? The shadows....they're real, aren't they?" "Yes, they are as well as devils that dominate this place." He answered, staring up at the sky. It was becoming darker every minute. "De...demons?" Simone stammered. "Yes. They are the ones who rule the darkness. And everything else around here."

"How do you know this?" She refused to trust whatsoever he was telling her. Shadows were one thing but demons? "I've been here longer than you have. I observe and I remember." He remarked, pointing his forefinger to his temple.

Simone's eyes widen. "You...You are M. You are the one who has been sending me letters." She remarked in bewilderment. The man only grinned slightly. "You instructed me to remember yet I don't know what I should remember." "Demons, they may take away your memory. You must've seen or heard something they didn't want you to know." He answered ruefully. Simone gulped. The missing bits of her recollections, they had been wiped away exactly like the ripped pages of her journal. As reality dawned on her she stepped back in horror. Her legs felt weak. It made sense. If the shadows were real then this all could be true as well. "The lady......the one in red." She whispered. The guy's eyes expand as he glanced at her. "You remember?" "No, but I can't hear out of my brain. I saw her. Not her face but her behind outside the Mayor's office." Simone replied, pushing the heels of her palms on her temples.

"Listen to me." The man said, suddenly fairly close and seeming afraid. "You have to remember. You have to discover a means to preserve your memories intact. Don't trust anybody." "Not even you?" "No, not even me." He warned. "Listen, I'm Matthew Brown. I used to live in the home you have moved into. My parents...Tom and Martha Brown." He gulped at their names and closed his eyes. Simone could see real agony on his face. "They were slain by the demons three years ago. I.....I...couldn't see their faces but I heard their words." He muttered dolorously as his gray eyes probed Simone's. "Oh my God." She whispered. "You have to find out something." He stated with urgency this time. " All this has been going on for years and will keep occurring if we won't stop them." "But how will I find out who they are?" "Start with the lady in red. And trust no one. No one." He whispered, putting his hands on her shoulders and squeezing them. "You are terrifying me." It was all Simone could say before Matt took a couple of steps back and peered behind them. His eyes were wild and his face pallid.

"Shadows. They are here. It can't be." He gasped as they both gazed at the shadows rushing into the jungle. "They must've been keeping an eye out for you. Run. I don't know whether I'd be able to assist you much further." With these remarks, he shoved Simone back and fled. He was moving deeper into the woods. Simone watched him depart, her heart beating in her breast as the sky got darker above and the shadows closed in behind her. Simone let out a scream. She was terrified, fatigued, and feeling hopeless.

Breathing raggedly, Simone turned to peer at the shadows. They weren't there. There was nothing around her except black trees. The sun had set and there was no light to cast shadows. Taking a deep breath, she started her way back towards her home. She stopped short in her steps as she found Jenna there, waiting for her. She was resting against her automobile parked in front of her home. She was clothed in a white button-down shirt over black pants. She was looking the other way as she spun her vehicle keys around her finger. As if feeling her there, she turned to gaze at Simone. "Where were you?" She asked, eyes narrowing. Simone shrugged and headed for her house. "Hey, I asked you something." "I was just around. Why are you here?" "I wanted to talk to you, mind if I come inside?" She asked, her face giving no clue as to what she wanted from Simone. Sighing loudly and facing her, Simone shook her head. "Sorry, mom has guests over and whatever you need to say can be said here." Jenna sneered, "I don't know what's so fantastic about you that both Brianna and Nathan can't quit talking about you." "Jenna, why are you here?" Simone bit out the words, impatient to get inside. In the safety of her bedroom. Or maybe she wasn't safe even there.

"Is this page yours?" She said, revealing a folded piece of paper she had in her hand. It was light blue in color. The same color her diary was. The color drained from Simone's face as she reached for it. "Where did you get this?" She whispered. "It was in my locker. I know your handwriting therefore I realized that it was yours straight immediately." Jenna shrugged. Carefully, Simone opened the page and went for the street light to read. She couldn't walk more than three steps. There were shadows. A few of them below the light. "You know, thank you." She told Jenna nervously as she ran towards the main door. Inside, she heard the women conversing and laughing. As she ran up the steps, she could hear the clinking of glasses. It was going to be a long night, she thought. On top of the steps, she felt something chilly around her ankles. When she peered down, she gasped. A shadow. Or a hand of a shadow. Wrapped around her ankle. Stifling a scream, she pulled her ankle and fled into the dark corridor as soon as she felt it release go. She dodged inside Jayden's room which was dark for he was down with her mother. Catching her breath, she peered out in the hallway to seek the shadow. Sure enough, it was still there on top of the steps. Waiting. Despite being afraid, Simone knew something. Of course, the shadows could not form where there was no light. They could never follow her into the regions with no lighting. She laughed skittishly. Why couldn't she think of it sooner? Straightening her shoulders, she flung open her bedroom door and strode inside.

Her confidence fled as soon as she glanced at the condition of her room. The light from the street lights filled her chamber but that was not what stole her breath away. Shadows were creeping all over the place. They dispersed like ants as she came in. Within a flash of an eye, they were gone. Simone knew, she knew that if Matthew had been honest then she would forget this recollection. The memory of meeting Matthew and shadows on the stairs as well as her room. She glanced down at the paper in her hand. It was exactly like every other page from her journal with nothing special about it. At least not what Simone wanted.

Throwing the paper aside, she pulled out her phone and slammed open her closet. She knew that she could fit inside just fine. With one peek at her room from over her shoulder, Simone went into the closet and locked its doors behind her. It was tough to sit in there. With so much clothing hanging, it was hard to breathe for her. But she needed to do it. She needed to capture all she had observed on her phone. With her phone being on her all the time, no one was going to remove those files. With no shadows in the closet, she was confident that no one would know about her filming everything. For safety precautions, she wrote about her day in her daily notebook and carefully put it on her table. For the devils to discover. That night, she positioned the camera between her books on the rack. Facing it in a manner that it recorded the area surrounding her bed.

The next morning, she woke up with her head feeling like a rock on her shoulders. She did not recall when she had gone to sleep. She couldn't recall anything beyond fixing supper with her mother. Before she could sit up, Jayden barged into her room. "Please tell me that you have my images from the vacation this summer." He said, collapsing on the bed and virtually on her. "Ow! Watch it, bozo!" Simone yelled out. "Please, please tell me that you have those images!!" He implored. Rolling her eyes, Simone whacked him on the head. "I transferred those photographs on your tab before removing them from the camera. What did you do?" She questioned him curiously. "I unintentionally factory reset the tab." He replied, biting his bottom lip. Simone felt as if he was going to weep any second now. "Accidently or purposely?" Simone responded. "Does it matter?" "Yes, it does. Now I will have to recover the data from the camera's memory card. It's a headache and my head is already hurting me. I feel like I haven't eaten in days!" She replied, blazing holes into her younger sibling. His shoulders slumped as he continued staring at her. Instantly, Simone felt horrible for yelling at him. "Look, after breakfast, I promise that I will recover the pictures from the card. Ok?" Jayden grinned and raced out of the room after giving her a brief embrace. Shaking her head, she proceeded to get ready for breakfast.

"So dad, you are not working today?" She questioned her father who was on his third cup of coffee as he read the newspaper. Lately, he appeared disturbed. She wanted to make it out that it was meant to be a joyous start but he was disturbed immediately. Jayden was having problems making friends at school and Simone was losing portions of her memories. She had informed her parents about it only this morning and they had exchanged a look of worry but had said nothing. "It's Sunday. Why would I work on Sunday?" He asked, putting a palm over his heart in feigned distress. "You were working on Saturday," Simone said, snorting. "The position I've been hired for, it had been vacant for three long years. Imagine the job." Her father remarked, letting out an audible sigh. "That reminds me when I came over to bring you the lunch box, I spotted a lady. I couldn't see her face because she was clothed in crimson. Had long sleek hair." Simone inquired, twisting her fork in the noodles. "Ah, Madam Mayor. She frequently dresses in crimson or black." Her father replied, appreciation obvious in his voice. "What...what type of lady is she?" "She is a really nice person. Gorgeous and courteous. She generally arrives in the late afternoon with her lover and they work until late at night." Her father remarked, sipping the leftover coffee in his cup. "Oh. Cool." Simone whispered as her father caressed her hair as he exited the room.

It took roughly one hour to retrieve all the data from the memory card. All the time, Jayden had lurked behind her and thrice she had to urge him to quit talking. The camera had not been used since Jayden's vacation so when three movies showed up beside his images, Simone scowled. They dated since after they had relocated to Elmdale. She couldn't recall recording any.

Handing over the files to Jayden, Simone clicked up the first video. Her mouth fell at what she witnessed. Shadows entered her chamber joined by a lady as she slept. The lady was clothed in crimson. Even though she had her back to the camera, Simone could tell that it was the mayor. She saw, horrified, as the woman bent over her and then headed for the camera. She had no clue what she had done to her. When she raised the camera to do something with it, perhaps delete the film, Simone gasped and sprang up so rapidly that her chair tumbled to the floor. Her blood had gone ice cold and her legs were shivering. The lady in the video was someone she knew. It was Brianna Hoskin.

CHAPTER 4

Simone avoided everyone at the school the following day. Trust no one. No one. Just before bed last night, she had come discovered her recording on her phone. She had documented her encounter with a man called Matthew Brown. The man from the woods. He had urged her to be cautious. Her lost memories, shadows, and her interaction with Matthew made sense but her mind refused to trust any of it.

At school, Simone observed that Brianna was missing and so were her pals. Where might they be? She pondered as she moved from one class to another for the lectures. Nathan had attempted to chat with her a few times but she had avoided him. She felt horrible for treating her one friend that way but the warning made it difficult for her to trust him.

When it was off time, she walked directly to the town's library. The structure was enormous and historic. Taking a big breath, she flung open the door and walked inside. There was no one there. Close a few on the second level on the table just near the railing. They were giggling about something they were reading from a book. At the bottom level, it was silent. Librarian was engaged in reading some type of magazine.

"Hey..." Simone cleared her throat. Librarian was a middle-aged lady wearing half-moon glasses on her tiny nose. She curled her tiny lips, painted crimson, towards Simone as though she was displeased with her existence there. Her brilliant blue eyes narrowed as she observed Simone. "Oh, you are the new girl." The lady placed the magazine down and clapped loudly. Simone lifted her eyebrow at her dubiously. "Ah..yes. I am." "How can I assist you, darling?" The librarian chirped. Simone stared at the tag placed on the woman's breast pocket. Samantha Markson. "Umm, I was wondering whether there'd be anything on Elmdale at the library." "Oh baby, there isn't much." She remarked with a wink as she begins tapping keys on the computer keyboard. "Why? Isn't this town old?" "It is however not many people stay here. The oldest in Elmdale is a lady aged fifty-four atm. Rest simply leave. Without a word. I believe that the tradition here or whatever." She said with a giggle. "What....?" Simone murmured. What does she mean by people simply leaving? "Surprising, I know. I don't know who began the tradition but practically everyone leaves a written message behind for their loved ones before going off abruptly." Ms. Markson carried on, without glancing at Simone's pale face. Did she even comprehend what she was saying? Why would 'everyone' abandon the town like that?

"Ah, found it. Just a few newspaper articles from the prior several years, nothing new. You could discover something intriguing because I haven't checked that folder for forever. Elmdale is a little town and almost anybody knows about it. Except for the folks who actually know how to look." Ms. Markson laughed, making a grimace at no one in particular. Simone scarcely listened to her because her mind was still thinking about the new piece of knowledge she had now. "Here." Ms. Markson scrawled something on a post-it note and passed it back to Simone. "To be honest, I'm shocked that you want to know about this place. No one, in my tenure of eight years here, has inquired for the things on Elmdale." "Guess there is always a first time for everything," Simone remarked, gazing at the letter. Ms. Markson had specified the floor, rack, and row of the area containing the old newspapers. Mumbling thanks, she walked upstairs. Sunlight streamed through the old windows of the buildings and illuminated the top floor. Hesitating, Simone gazed around for the shadows. She had yet to see them during the day but given the current change of events, she had to keep an eye out. She moved towards the furthest corner, away from the pair on the floor. As she went, she kept looking at the shelves and the rare collection of thousands of books. For a little village, Elmdale undoubtedly has its collection of books.

At the farthest corner, where the sunlight shone best, was a stand with a giant folder on top of it. It was encrusted in the dust. Quietly and neatly, Simone brushed it off and opened it. She breathed a little more loudly than required and attempted to calm herself. Her heart was racing frantically with anticipation and anxiety. The earliest newspaper clipping was dated back a century. When the town came into existence. 1908! It featured a few photographs that faded with time with descriptions of the place. It was a little one. The following few papers informed her about the festivities, celebrations, and few individuals making it big from Elmdale in politics and sports. Nothing worth noting here, Simone thought as she scanned over the pages. At practically the end she came across a piece of information that drew her attention. A couple unexpectedly departed from Elmdale. A little settlement north of Newland. Below the headline, the reporter had highlighted additional persons who had gone missing since the town came in 1908. There was a total of eighteen persons missing at the end of 1936. 'The disappearance of the people of Elmdale's continues even after decades. They depart without a trace. The police and the mayor, Mr. Jason Breckon are worried over this delicate subject.'

There was nothing after that. Confused, Simone looked through all the pages again but there was nothing. At the very end, a newspaper from a decade ago reported that approximately sixty people had gone missing in Elmdale but the administration was very quiet about it. 'I'd like to think that the folks simply go. Move out from the town, leaving their loved ones behind.' The mayor had remarked in an interview. 'The police and the government have been working on the cases of missing individuals for a century but have discovered no trace. The only reason that makes it logical that we have settled on before concluding the case is, that people move on. Elmdale is not a huge town like all other towns and cities out there in the globe therefore I don't believe many people regret leaving.' He had failed to recognize the subsequent arguments offered by the people in the years that followed. There was nothing after that. Nothing at all. But the individuals were still going missing.

Simone was so interested in the new knowledge that she totally overlooked the darkness sweeping around the library. When she felt chilly, she pulled up her head to gaze about her. Shadows. They were crawling through the bookcases and on the walls. She gasped as she felt something chilly and slithery on her palm. Shadows were creeping out of the folder she had been reading. What the heck was this? It was her first time seeing them during the day. She took faltering steps back, her scream trapped in her throat. A gasp escaped her lips when she connected with a book rack, sending a few volumes crashing down from the top shelf. The sound of the books dropping on the cold hard floor of the library made the shadows halt for a time. They seemed solid. Now that Simone could see them more clearly, she saw that they looked to be in varying shades of black. Some were large and some were little. Some were deformed and some looked fine. They appeared genuine. They looked to be breathing. In a manner. They radiated eeriness, something that made Simone's heart make frantic spasms. She closed her eyes as they all came closer. Blocking the vista behind them to her dismay. Solid. Is this the end? She thought as a chill crept up her body and she felt the whisper of the shadows' touch.

"Simone? What are you doing here?" Simone jerked open her eyes at the sound. She glanced about her furiously and felt herself to check whether she was harmed. No, she was fine and the shadows were gone. As though they hadn't been there. "Hey, you ok?" The voice inquired again, anxious this time. Simone glanced up to discover that it was Nathan. His brow was pinched with anxiety as he gazed at Simone and around her. "What happened?" He questioned, leaning nearer her. "Ahh...." Simone stroked her head, thinking fiercely. "I thought I heard a mouse.....I...uh...jumped back and collided into the rack...Ummm the books fell and I was scared...that...that...the rack will fall and I'd be trapped underneath it." She concluded, nodding and oddly pleased with her apology. Nathan merely lifted his eyebrows at her.

"What...what are you doing here?" She questioned him who was now gathering up the books that had dropped down on the floor. "I come here a lot. It's the only area that I love to be in." He remarked, winking at her. After he was done organizing the books, he raked his fingers through his hair uncomfortably. "So, anything I can assist you with around here?" "No...no. Thank you. I was just...just headed home now." Simone remarked, making her way towards the stairs. Her legs felt weak and she pushed herself to seem calm. Nathan followed her without a word. Downstairs, someone was busy talking with the librarian. Simone could hear her giggle quietly all over to the stairs at the far left of the level.

"Kyle!! Need to stay?" Nathan screamed out to the man from behind Simone, moving past her towards the main desk. "Nah, dude. I simply followed you here." His pal responded, his voice thick as he grinned at the librarian. "You're headed home?" Nathan turned to ask Simone. She opened her lips to say yes but then decided against it. "Why?" "If you have time, we can go someplace fun?" He offered, a dimpled grin on his face. Trust no one. No one. Matthew's cautionary words reverberated in her thoughts as she glanced at the two youngsters waiting impatiently for her response. "Yeah, I have a little time to walk about. Where do you have in mind?" She inquired and shuddered a bit as Kyle smacked Nathan on the back, sending the poor guy sliding a couple of steps forward. "Just around the bend. The gambling station." Nathan said, smiling from ear to ear. Behind him, Kyle was rolling his eyes but she could detect a glimmer of the grin on his face too. Simone saw that he was one of the individuals that Nathan hung out with most regularly at school. He had shoulder-length brown hair and he was taller than Nathan. Some three to five inches. He even appeared to be older than them. "Isn't that the guys' thing?" Simone said, shaking her head at the idea of boys playing the weird fighting games. "Not really. It's the only area near here where the youngsters hang out regularly. You'd be astonished to see more chicks than boys." Nathan said as they started moving towards the library doors. Trust no one. No one. Simone remembered the warning once again.

"Uh...

Do you mind if I drop by my place and change my clothes?" She asked the lads. They both turned around to look at her, then at each other before Nathan nodded. "Thanks. I'll see you here in a few." Simone waved at them uncomfortably and ran towards her bike. Under no circumstances she was going to risk losing her memories of what she had read and witnessed. Like Matthew had stated, she could trust no one. Not even Nathan who had been her only good friend for the month she had been here.

Just outside her house, once again she found Jenna waiting for her. Sighing, Simone walked up to her. "Now, what are you doing here?" She growled out. Jenna only grimaced at her before dragging her arm towards the main entrance. "Whoa wait. What are you doing?" Simone attempted to extricate her hand but failed. "I need to talk to you. Asap!" "We can chat here." "No, we can't. I don't want the darkness to discover us." Jenna winked as Simone's eyes widen in surprise. Jenna seemed pleased with herself. She did not appear like she was kidding. Simone glanced about her, terrified that someone could have overheard them but the street was clear. No one was outdoors or even in the windows. "I...I don't know what you are talking about." Simone murmured, her heart thumping painfully in her chest. Jenna's lips twisted in a teasing grin towards her. "Did you truly believe you are the only person in quest for the answers?" "Look, Jenna, I don't know what you are getting at here," Simone remarked, attempting to step past Jenna but she stopped her. "I've got to be someplace."

"I lost my mom a year ago. That is when I recognized that there was something wrong with this community. I began seeing odd things." Jenna murmured, her voice quiet and sadness clear from her features. "Please, may we speak inside?" Simone didn't know what to do. Trust no one. No one. The words went on resonating in her thoughts. At last, she gave up and summoned Jenna over. Her father was at work and Jayden was building some type of project model for his school. Her mother smiled when she saw Jenna with Simone. "Wonderful to see you my darling. What would you like? Ice cream or cold coffee?" "Ice cream maybe?" Jenna smiled, making her mother giggle.

In her bedroom, Simone maintained her distance from her. The movies on her phone which she had obtained from the camera revealed that Brianna had required physical contact with her to wipe her memories away. She was not going to provide an opportunity to Jenna to do the same unless she was lying about everything simply to have Simone believe her. They merely spoke about their studies and classmates as they waited for Simone's mother to bring in the ice cream. "I'm genuinely astonished to find that Nathan spends too much time with you.

Mostly he simply remains miles away from ladies despite them pursuing him throughout the campus." Jenna was saying as she toyed with her ice cream in the cup. It was going to melt and destroy her clothing. "Look, I don't know what people think but I didn't ask him to follow me around. Heck, I didn't even give him any type of initiative." "Well, it is the precise thing that attracted him. He is a great person, you know. Nicer than lots of folks surrounding this place." Jenna slurped on her ice cream, making Simone gape at her. That was one strange method of eating ice cream. When they were done, Jenna wrapped her dark red hair into a bun at the back of her neck and flung open Simone's closet doors. "Come on. We can't take chances." "Jenna, whatever you've got to say, do it here. I'm NOT going to go into the closet with you." Simone responded, putting her arms over her chest stubbornly. Sighing, Jenna closed the closet doors and walked to draw the drapes over the windows. She closed the door and every location from whence the sunset sunshine spilled through. She switched off the light, generating semi-darkness within the room.

"As I mentioned, I lost my mum last year. She didn't vanish, she was killed." She started, sitting down on Simone's bed. Simone took the chair near the table. "I was at home when it happened. I... When I heard my mom scream, I hurried up the stairs. I hammered on her bedroom door which was locked. I have to break it in. That is when I discovered her corpse. She was emptied of blood. Strange, right?" She questioned Simone, clutching a cushion close. "Look, if you are going to tell me there are vampires in this down then I'm not going to believe you. I mean, what do you want me to think?" Simone remarked exasperatedly, throwing up her hands. She should've realized that bringing Jenna around was a horrible, very bad idea. "Simone, I know. I know that you've lost your memories and you see them. You see the shadows but you don't recall seeing them. The devils. They control the shadows. This town, they rule over it." Jenna said, trying to keep her voice upbeat. She was looking unseeingly at the floor. Simone didn't know what to say to her. "Unlike you, I have some wisdom to remain off their radar." "Or immediately beneath it," Simone murmured. Jenna let out a humorless and self-disparaging chuckle. "You know about Brianna. I'm impressed. It took me months to find the truth about her." "Aren't you scared of her?" Simone asked her. Jenna shook her head and looked at her. "No, I'm terrified of the genius behind her. Demons obey someone. Someone I have yet to find out. Someone who is onto you" She whispered the latter part, her fearful eyes looking at Simone.

CHAPTER 5

Simone's mouth fell. "What are you talking about?" "You know that I'm close to Brianna. I follow her occasionally. Keeping a safe space between us of course. I saw her....once talking with someone I couldn't see the face. It was a man, at the mayor's office. She is terrified of him. She obeys him." Jenna was saying, her voice barely above a whisper. Simone was perplexed. "And how is that guy chasing me?" "I heard your name. He mentioned your name. That is all." "It is also conceivable that Brianna reports everything to him?" Simone suggested and Jenna agreed, nibbling on her bottom lip. "Simone, when individuals vanish they dispose of their stuff. Their books end up at the library. I went there several times but Brianna became suspicious so I stopped but not before I got my hands on some actual goods." Jenna concluded with a wink.

"Real stuff?" Simone asked dryly. "Yeah. Since you walked inside the library today, I know that you must've studied the town's history." "So, you're spying on me?" Simone exclaimed, unable to keep the venom from her voice. "God, can you stop being hostile towards me already?" "Look, given the circumstances, I don't trust you," Simone replied, running her fingers through her hair. "What if you are one of....of those creatures out there? How would I know?" "Seriously?" Jenna muttered, tightening her jaw. "Fine, don't believe but I've had to tell you everything before is too late." "Everything?" "Yeah. As you must've read, all this is going on for roughly a century. Even when the town came into. What I learned, is that the darkness and demons have been here longer than that." Jenna replied, tossing a little worn-out journal at Simone at the catch.

"Wait, what?" "In 1964, there was this man who got fortunate. Like many others throughout the century, he had realized that something was strange about this area but unlike the others, he had managed to remain alive for the time being." Simone sucked at her bottom lip as she opened the journal. She could see untidy handwriting written on the yellow pages. She was frightened that the paper might rip into pieces only at her touch. "What happened to him?" She muttered, fingering the words. "Which happens to everyone else who attempts to come too near to the truth," Jenna said regretfully, glancing down at her intertwined fingers. "Oh." "So, this person indicated that the existence of these animals he called demons went back to before the town came into. They are the product of a curse." Jenna said. "Oh great, a curse now. What's next? Aladdin's magic lamp?" Simone blurted out, instantly regretting the words that had left her lips. Jenna looked hurt. "Simone, I'm trying to help." "Fine, go ahead."

"Unfortunately, the guy couldn't find out about the origins of the curse or anything else about it. Though, he did note in his diary that these beings are tied to something. This means something is keeping them in here. In this town. I also pondered why they aren't spotted outside the town, why in Elmdale so when I saw the diary, this explanation made sense." Jenna continued continuing as Simone was leafing over the pages attentively. She scanned through the notes and she could see that the man had seen worse. She wondered how he had managed to not go crazy.

"Does this material also informs about what to do to get rid of them?" She asked, well conscious of her running out of time. Nathan and Kyle must be waiting for her. "Be patient, I'm getting there." "Be fast since Nathan and Kyle will be here any minute now. I purchased a few minutes to change my clothing before hanging around for a bit." "Wow," Jenna said, blinking at her. Simone wasn't sure of what to make of her response. "Anyway, if this man is accurate about his claims then that implies if we identify that specific object that links these animals to the town, by eliminating it we can get rid of them.
The question is, where are we going to discover it and how?" "That's all?" "Getting this much was hazardous enough Simone. Learn to enjoy a little." "Fine, nice work. What more do you want me to do?" She questioned, rapidly growing through her clothing in the closet. She

could not decide. "Help me. Help me put things right or this will keep on occurring forever." Jenna begged behind her. "Did you also know that you can't leave the town now? Like ever?" She said regretfully. Simone stilled. Recalling the warning from the elderly man the day they had moved into Elmdale. "What?" She croaked out the word. "What did you say?" "Whoever attempts to leave Elmdale after living here disappears." Jenna sounded gloomy now. "There is no going back therefore there's got to be someone to take the initiative and annihilate these things."

"You're....you're correct." Simone nodded, lying down on her bed. "And two persons are much better than one. Together, we can find out more." Jenna was saying. She stretched out to grasp Simone's hand. "Ah yeah. Ok." "So, are you going to share what you know?" Jenna inquired sweetly, squeezing Simone's hand before letting go. Simone's mind was churning, pulling together what she knew. Or she believed she knew. "I don't know much." She murmured. Compared to Jenna, she truly had nothing on her. "I just found out about Brianna and....wait.

Do you know the Browns? The people who lived in this house?" She questioned, turning to face Jenna completely. "Of course, I do. They disappeared. But I know that they were killed. Why?" Jenna was perplexed. "Their son, Matthew Brown. Did he die too?" "I don't know, Simone. I truly don't." Jenna answered sorry as she gazed at Simone. "I met him," Simone remarked listlessly. "You....you what?" Jenna rose, her eyes wide and mouth gaping. "How is that possible? Browns were killed three years ago." "Believe me when I say that he is alive. He's been living in the woods." Hoping that she could recall her interaction with Matthew. All she knew was via the recording. "Oh my God. Tell me everything." And so Simone did. Somehow she knew that Jenna was correct. She could not cope with this all alone. She needed someone to depend on. After she was done, Jenna held her head in her hands. Before she could utter a word, the house bell sounded. It was Nathan.

"Look, I gotta leave. We'll chat more." Simone muttered and she swiftly changed her top into whatever her hands grabbed from the closet.

Jenna was still shaking her head. "We'll have to meet up again. So many times I wish that we had phone service in this town." She whispered as she watched Simone pull her long hair into a ponytail. She did not want her mother to go and answer the door for she did not want Nathan or Kyle to know that Jenna had been at her home. "We will." She promised Jenna and hurried towards the main door. Thankfully, her mother was in the kitchen with headphones on while Jayden was nowhere to be seen.

When she walked out, Nathan and Kyle were there. Both were riding their bikes. "Took you long enough," Kyle commented. "It's ok. No haste." Nathan stated after throwing a peek at Kyle. Without a word, Simone hopped aboard her bike, and her gaze focused on the woodland in front of them. Further ahead, the jungle was still gloomy beneath the blazing afternoon light. "You ok?" Nathan yelled back to her when he discovered that she was not moving. "Yeah, I'm....I'm OK." Nathan remained to stare at her when she joined them on the road and then he glanced back at the trees. Simone knew she'd loathe whatever concept he'd come up with the minute he opened his lips. "You know what, let's go there." He remarked mischievously, tilting his head back towards the jungle. "You know we can't, smartie pants." Simone shot back at the same moment as Kyle snapped, "No way, guy!"

"What? Learn to live a little Kyle. Come on, Simone. Don't tell me that you're terrified." He tormented her, making her moan in anger. Deep down she wanted to go but she was terrified too. "Nathan..!!" Kyle remarked warningly but his pal disregarded him. Leaving his bicycle just outside the gate of Simone's home, he smirked at the two of them. "Let's have a race. The one to reach....." Even before he could finish, Simone took off. She disregarded when Nathan mockingly accused her of cheating and Kyle screamed to implore her to come back. There was no going back now. She wanted to see the forest.

Simone ran. Branches snugged at her clothes and the twigs shattered under her feet but she did not stop. She could sense that Nathan was close behind her. The trees began to thin out almost quickly. Surprised, Simone paused halfway because there was an open space in front of her. Behind her, Nathan also came to a halt. Both of them were breathing heavily. While Simone glanced at everything around them, Nathan bowed down with his hands on his knees as he took deep breaths.

"Ok, you won." He rasped. "Nathan, look." She whispered instead. Just ahead of an open area, there was a rocky slope that soared even higher than the tallest tree in the forest or so Simone believed. "Wow...Truth be told, I've never been this deep in the forest before." He murmured as he made careful steps towards what seemed to be a cave at the foot of the hill. "Nathan, be cautious." She shouted out to him but he waved his hand at her from over his shoulder. Just then, Kyle came behind them, looking like a furious bull. His long hair hand twigs and dried leaves. He looked funny enough to send Simon into convulsions of laughter. "Oh, God. I wish I could show you the way you appear right now." She remarked, pointing at his hair. "Wait until you see where you've come, you fool." He snarled out in answer. Simone's laughter evaporated at his words.

"Kyle, stop up guy! Don't be a coward." Nathan yelled out to them, encouraging Simone to join him. She paused, remembering her previous visit to the woodland. What was she thinking? What if she made these people run into Matthew? She had intended to lose the lads in the forest and then wait for them to return without her but they had followed her. Almost too perfectly. Suddenly, Simone's throat felt dry and her heart thudded in her chest. When they were silent, they could hear the wind moan through the trees. Just as she looked, the shadows of the trees got darker. Soon enough, she could see them moving up on the hill where the sunshine was the greatest. They had appeared twice in one day. During the day. What was happening? "Nathan!!!! WE NEED TO LEAVE!!" Kyle yelled at his companion, not glancing up at the shadows above them. Could he see them? Simone thought numbly. "A sec..."

They heard Nathan say. "NATHAN!!" She yelled his name as the hill above them began to darken with darkness. Just how many were there? "Oh my God." Beside Simone, Kyle muttered. His gaze was fixated on where Nathan had vanished. Mist or fog. It was one of those things and it was spreading rapidly. Nathan was nowhere to be seen. "NATHAN!!!" Simone and Kyle yelled together. "RUN!!" They heard Nathan yell before he arrived from the fog. He was hobbling and his forehead was plastered with perspiration beads. "RUN AS FAST AS YOU CAN!" "WHAT THE HELL IS THIS?" Simone yelled out at him all the while fighting Kyle's grasp on her arm. "Mist. It'll make you numb." Nathan was saying, his breathing heavily as he had problems walking. Jerking his hand away, Simon raced to aid him. Cold.

The mist felt chilly around her ankles much as the shadows were. She trembled but the drive to assist Nathan prevailed over whatever she was experiencing. "Let's go." She replied, grabbing his arm and slinging it over her shoulders. Nathan pulled back from her. When he held her shoulders to make her face him, she could see that his face was crimson with anguish. Why couldn't she feel anything? She pondered. "Just. Go." With these words, he pushed her aside. She stared, frightened as the cloud took him completely. She let out a cry as Kyle started pulling her away. A few steps later, they burst into a sprint. She rushed as quickly as she could, avoiding the rough branches smacking her face. She was convinced that she had a couple of wounds on her face and her hands were bleeding.

Soon, they were out of the trees. Kyle halted a few steps ahead of her. He, too, was breathing hard but otherwise looked to be in much better shape than Simone was. Nathan wasn't there. Was......was he... "He is not coming back, is he?" Kyle questioned her in nearly a whisper. Simone felt a massive knot in her throat and she did not trust herself to speak. "What's going on here?" She turned at Jenna's angry voice behind her. So she hadn't left when Simone had. "Nathan......Nathan...he...he recommended going..." Simone halted, not trusting herself to continue. "Stupid jerk!" Kyle murmured, pushing the heels of his palms into his temples. "Simone, what happened?" Jenna questioned once again, her questioning glance meeting Simone's. "Nathan...I suppose he is gone." It was all Simone could say. Jenna gasped as Kyle kicked a stone in fury. What were they going to do now? Was Nathan truly gone? What precisely had transpired back there? Too many questions muddled Simone's head. When Kyle began walking away, his shoulders sagging and head down, Simone lost all the optimism she had. "What....should we...are we meant to tell anyone?" Simone questioned Jenna, not aware that she was holding at her t-shirt too firmly. Jenna tried to hold her at an arm's distance and shook her once to get her all attention. "Were the shadows there?" She asked Simone. Gulping, Simone nodded and told her about the mist. "Then the demons will take care of the matter. Don't worry." Jenna had stated. When she had pulled Simone back to her home, the sun had nearly set behind them. When Jenna instructed Simone to get into bed, she agreed. She was too fatigued and had informed her mother that she was coming down with the flu or something. She was left alone to recuperate.

"After what occurred today, I'm sure Brianna or someone else will come to take away your memory of today," Jenna murmured, going down to face Simone who was laying upright and stared unseeingly at the roof. "Let them come. I want to forget. It is my fault. It is." Simone sobbed and bit her cheek to keep herself from crying. She could taste blood. "No, it wasn't your fault," Jenna whispered and proceeded to take out Simone's camera. Turning it on, she positioned it amid her clothing in the closet in such a manner that it faced the bed. Simone would've liked it all any other day but not now. Not at all. Nathan was gone. She was the one for whom he had recommended going to the forest. It was her fault. Only hers.

Simone opened her eyes to the sounds of birds singing outside her bedroom window. Surprised, she flung back the blankets and hurried to look. Throwing open the window, she gasped at what she saw. Birds. Loads and lots of them soaring from above the Elmdale. What was happening? What had made them fly away from the forest? With her eyes wide, she glanced towards the woodland on her left. Suddenly she remembered the happenings of the day before. Her legs fell out under her and she sank to the window seat. Nathan was gone. There had been a mist and... She hurried towards the closet, remembering the camera Jenna had put there. The camera was still there, filming precisely as Jenna had set it up. What had happened? Why hadn't she forgotten the memories? She paused the video and then played it.

Brianna had come. Simone could see her on the camera, standing near her bed. She was clothed in total black but her face was revealed. She was sporting vivid red lipstick. When she was ready to kneel oversleeping Simone, she sprang back in surprise. Someone else had entered the room. Simone's throat got dry as she saw Brianna's face. The demon's jaw was hanging open and her eyes were wide. "What are you doing here? Why did you come here?" The camera caught her voice. "Leave her alone, Quinlynn." Said a guy's voice. She could not see him. He must've stood near the entrance. "Why? Why should I let her be?" Brianna had snapped. "Because she is mine." The deep voice had answered. Simone gasped as the camera slid from her hands and onto her bed.

CHAPTER 6

She hurried to Jenna's. Her feet hardly touched the floor. She had scarcely heard her mother summoning her for breakfast. When she reached her friend's home, she hammered on the door. An elderly man opened it up as she was between knocks. He certainly seemed upset. "Jenna, she hasn't gone to school, has she?" Simone rasped, inhaling deeply. Before she could receive a reply, Jenna was there. "Simone, you ok? What...what are you doing here so early in the morning and......." She paused when she spotted the camera in Simone's hand. Suddenly she grew tight and rigid. "Come...come on in. Gramps, I have something incredibly essential to speak concerning our history assignment before school, ok?" Jenna notified her grandpa and pulled Simone into the home. She didn't let go of her hand as they climbed up the stairs and into Jenna's room. Simone didn't even pause and thrust the camera towards Jenna. Without a word, they re-watched the footage. Jenna's hands trembled at the point when Simone had dropped the camera. "Yours?" Brianna had chewed out the words. "Leave, Quinlynn." The deep voice had demanded. The video concluded with Brianna slipping into the thin air.

"This...this is...I told you." Jenna remarked, putting away the camera. "What..what do we do now? I mean...I...uh...what did I ever accomplish to gain his attention? Whoever it is." Simone replied, massaging her forearms to fight off the cold. "I don't know Simone, I truly don't," Jenna murmured back, still clutching the camera. Nodding, Simone got back her camera and headed for her residence to get ready for the day at school.

"Where have you been? Is everything ok?" Her father questioned her right outside the front entrance. Seeing him all dressed for the office, Simone got an idea. It was time to confront whatever monsters lurked in the town. She didn't want to wait and be hunted. "Dad, I have a vital message for the mayor. Think you can drop it off at her office?" Her father lifted his eyebrow at her, his lips slightly ajar. "I mean, simply slide inside her office from beneath the door. You can do it, right?" Simone inserted hurriedly. "Honey, if there is any trouble about anything, you may speak to me or your mom." "No, everything is okay. It's only that there is something I want the mayor to know. I don't want others to find out. Yet." She remarked with a strained grin.

I've located Matthew Brown, son of Tom and Martha Brown. If you wish to meet him, come by Dawsons' home. Alone.

Simone didn't feel very secure after handing over the message to her father. Several times, she wanted to hurry to the mayor's office and grab the letter back from her father. Seeing Brianna act normal at school didn't help either now that she was alone. Nathan was gone. Everyone except saves two persons behaved as if everything was okay in the world. Kyle laughed and spoke with his pals. It was evident that he had forgotten all that had transpired in the forest yesterday. Everyone behaved as if Nathan Woods had never lived.

"This is crazy." Jenna had whispered to her in their literature class. Vanessa and Brianna had cast her a glance, apparently bewildered by the unexpected closeness between Simone and Jenna. When Simone opened her mouth to say more about the matter, Jenna elbowed her and then jerked her head subtly towards Brianna sitting just two seats away. Simone wanted to explain that there was no light and there were no shadows. How would Brianna know?

When Simone couldn't take anymore, she went to stand by Nathan's locker. It was her first time standing there. Before, it had always been Nathan waiting for her at her locker. It was unlocked. Simone opened it warily, glancing over her shoulders to check if anybody was gazing at her suspiciously. No one was. She was confident that everyone had forgotten about Nathan Woods. He had been obliterated from their memory. Simone clinched her mouth and glanced into the locker. It was vacant. It seemed as though it had been vacant forever. "I'm sorry, I can't do it." She murmured and raced out. No one stopped her as she rode back to her home.

Her parents were not at home so she let herself in and raced to her bedroom where she let her tears flow.

Simone waited for someone, anybody to come up beside the forest but no one did. Evening came in and her family was back. Jayden's endeavor had been a smash and he was nearly beaming. Her parents were pleased with him and had chosen to take them out for supper. "I don't want to leave. I'm exhausted." She had excused herself. "Simone, I found out that you were missing from a lot of your courses today." Her mother had remarked, tossing a yellow shirt at Jayden to change into. "Yeah, I felt terrible and didn't have it in me to go to the principal's office for the leave." She murmured. A falsehood slipping out readily.

Her parents appeared to have bought it which was why, an hour later she was alone at the home. She had shut out the lights of the whole house and had sat on the window seat of her bedroom. She waited. The ticking of the clock was the only thing she could hear. Distant sounds of laughter and dishes could barely be heard. Her eyes grew heavy as she waited. She was about to doze asleep when she heard it. Click, clack, click, clack... The sound of heels. It sounded familiar. Simone didn't move from her location. She was afraid that she'd cause a sound.

It was a woman. She stopped in front of the forest, her back to Simone's house. Swallowing, Simone ran. Towards the main entrance, to face her. To face Brianna or Quinlynn. Whatever her name was.

"Brianna!!" Simone called as she went out of her residence. Slowly, the lady turned around to look at her. Seeing her face to face made Simone's throat go dry. Beside her, the street light flickered. Without even turning to look, she knew that shadows were growing about them. "Well, well. Looks like our clever girl has caught me." Brianna stated. Her voice was icy cold which sent chills down Simone's spine. Around them, everything had stilled, or how Simone sensed it. She couldn't even feel the evening air blowing. "What do you....you want?" Despite herself, she stuttered. When Brianna laughed, her eyes sparked ember. "I want you to quit being so inquisitive. I've tried to make your life comfortable here but now you have made your own grave." Brianna stated as she began approaching Simone. She emanated confidence and shadows appeared to part ways with her. Simone swallowed and took a couple of unsteady steps back.

"You've....you've...been...killing people." Simone managed to say. Brianna laughed grimly. "Killing? Have you seen me murder, sweetheart?" "No, but I know. Everyone who vanishes – " "Well, your food does vanish when you eat it." Brianna cut in. "And then you throw away or bury the bones." At these words, Simone stopped breathing and her legs went out under her. Air whooshed out of her lungs as her back impacted the road. Brianna laughed boisterously. "You are brilliant, aren't you?" "What...what are you going to do to me?" Simone muttered, obviously shivering with anxiety. "What do you think? I hate being challenged and you've challenged me." Brianna said menacingly. Simone's heart hammered with hopeless, animal panic with every stride

Brianna made towards her. Simone peered behind Brianna, at the shadows waiting. Waiting for what? She did not know. She closed her eyes, dreading sending the message. Regretting everything. She stopped going back on her hands when she entered the middle of the shade cast by her home. Brianna had stopped walking at just the edge of the shadow.

"If you thought that you'd be safe from the shadows in the shadow, then I should give it to you that you do have common sense. Too bad, it got you here." "Go ahead.....kill....kill me," Simon murmured, glancing up at Brianna. "Awww..." Brianna cooed and then Simone felt herself being tugged. Alarmed, she sought to cling onto anything on the road but her fingers caught nothing. Her nails split and were gushing in seconds. She halted at Brianna's feet. A horrible grin was crossing on lips as she observed red drips fall on the road from Simone's fingernails. They bloody stung but Simone didn't want Brianna to know how much she was suffering. "Any final words, darling?" Brianna grinned excitedly, her ember eyes burning even brighter.

"Quinlynn!!!" A loud voice shouted behind them. Brianna's smile vanished as she took a step back from Simone to look. Behind her, someone was stepping out into the light from the shadow of the house. Someone Simone knew. "No...." She gasped as the light landed on Matthew's untamed curly hair. The moment the shadows evaporated at his presence and Brianna's shoulders dropped, Simone understood. Matthew had been the one. He had been the leader, the one the shadows and demons followed.

"Oh, is you. Fancy you turning up here." Brianna tittered, covering her lips with her pale palm. "You pushed my hand. I ordered you to leave the girl alone yet here you are." "You realize that she is an issue, right? Like all the others, we need to eliminate her." She said, pointing in Simone's direction from over her shoulder. Matthew just tilted his head. "I promised you that I would manage her." "I've always done your dirty job Trar'gen. Always. Why is it that this time I can't get my hands dirty?" "Because you've been careless and impatient. You didn't even know about Mathew Brown for three solid years." Matthew stated. Simone frowned. What was he saying? "You were there too, that night. You should've known about him if I didn't." Brianna fired back which made Matthew grin. A malevolent grin. "I did. I waited for you to recognize your error but you didn't." Matthew's comments were slipping out with a lazy glee. Nothing was making sense to Simone. She wanted to go back to her home, to the protection of her closet but as she attempted to take a step back, she jerked in surprise. Looking down, she gasped in terror. Shadows were pouring around her and clutching onto her legs. "And here you are, flaunting his face like a trophy after murdering him." Brianna chuckled mirthlessly which made Simone's skin tingle with anxiety.

"I had to since you were not capable of acknowledging your mistake from three years ago. I observed him speaking with my pal over there." Now, Matthew gazed up at Simone. Even though they were merely a few feet away, Simone could tell that his face had no warmth for her. "All the more incentive to get rid of this issue, right now and right now." Brianna intoned, touching Matthew's cheeks as if he were a youngster. Almost quickly, Simone felt the shadows slither up her legs. When she opened her mouth to scream, something cold silenced her. "I didn't say that you can do that," Matthew said softly. Brianna stilled and turned to face him. "What did you say?" "She is not yours to murder, Quinlynn. I genuinely appreciate all the hard work you did to tame her but I'd want you to give her over to me." Simone let out a strangled scream and shook her fiercely but the shadows were clutching onto her firmly. She couldn't feel her hands or legs anymore. "No. Never. I dislike it when you hold secrets from me, and do things out of usual. I know very well how it went the previous time." Brianna remarked, giving him a beautiful grin as she moved around him. Matthew only laughed in answer. "You know you can't fight me, Quinlynn. Give up." "Never, sweetie," Brianna muttered into his ear from over his shoulder before her eyes found Simone's. Simone couldn't breathe and she closed her eyes. Praying desperately. She felt herself being dragged effortlessly.

It all occurred like thunder flashing in the sky. One minute Simone was being strangled and frozen to death, the next instant she felt flung back. Horrified, she opened her eyes. Shadows were diving to capture her. Behind them, she could see Quinlynn, her face all scrunched in concentration. Simone let out a scream. She was going to strike the asphalt under her and perish. Just like that. "QUINLYNN!!" Somewhere near to her, Matthew yelled. His voice is utterly inhuman. Just before Simone could strike the earth, arms rushed out to catch her as easily as if she had slid not launched back into the air some good fifty feet. It was Matthew. He had rescued her. Before Simone could fathom what was unfolding around her, shadows closed in. She squirmed in Matthew's arms but he kept her tight. His hold was icy cold on her soft flesh. When the shadows created a blanket around them, she strained to breathe. Her lungs screamed at the lack of oxygen. She could not breathe. "Ma....ma..." She attempted to contact Matthew but failed. She gave up fighting then and accepted the darkness that filled her head.

Cold. She felt something chilly around her ankles and around her wrists. Shadows. She jerked open her eyes only to gasp in terror. She strained at her arms and legs but they didn't budge. She was tired down with an iron chain. On a chair. Thankfully, her mouth wasn't taped. She yelled. "SOMEONE!!" She called but heard no response. She had no idea how long she cried and screamed before she collapsed back into the chair, tired. Only then did she allow herself to investigate the room she was in. It was some type of cellar with a stairway only a foot behind her while a chair and a table graced the corner of the area. In the corner on Simone's right, there was a little bed. So she was locked up. Where? She did not know. With her head heavy and eyelids aching with all the crying and screaming, Simone let herself drift off to sleep.

When Simone came around again, she was lying down on something soft but she still could feel something cold around her ankle and wrist. She cursed and opened her eyes. "You're alive." She looked up at Matthew's voice. He was leaning against the table with his hands in his pants pockets. He appeared at ease yet officious at the same time. At the sound of his deep voice coming from the mouth of the boy she knew, she shuddered. "Where am I?" She managed to ask in a whisper, her eyes trained on the roof or what appeared to be. No, it wasn't the roof but the shadows. Shadows all across her head. "It's the facility where we store the people before murdering them off. People who are too problematic to bet allowed out in Elmdale." He answered quietly. "What do you intend on doing with me?" "As of now, nothing. What I am and what I desire, you will need time to be ready to listen to it all. I feel this is not the time." He said, his voice drifting away. "WELL, IT IS TIME YOU MONSTER," Simone yelled, facing the table but he was gone. There was no one. Above her, her shadows moved before becoming motionless again.

For the following several days or hours, she could not tell, Simone continued falling in and out of sleep. Sometimes she saw Matthew but he scarcely ever talked more than a word or two. He had liberated her wrist but one of her ankles was still shackled to the iron bed. Simone had attempted to move it but it didn't even budge. Simone was fed too. She never saw who delivered the food but she had her notions. All she saw in the room she was shadows. Everywhere. They never touched her but appeared to be keeping an eye on her. She had tried talking to them, yelling at them but it hardly elicited a response out of them. Then one day, Matthew delivered her meal tray personally.

"How long are you going to keep me here?" She questioned him, inspecting the meatballs and noodles on the platter. "Till you are ready to listen to me and trust me." He answered, his cool deep voice making her quiver. He was intimidating, no matter how innocuous he looked to be. There was this atmosphere surrounding him which made her feel that he wasn't someone she could mess with. "Look, you are keeping me shut up here with eerie shadows all around. If you want me to believe you and trust you then you are misguided." She fired back, shooting crumbs of her food from her mouthful. A disappointed grimace flashed across his face before it turned passive once again. "Did you know that we were formed with a curse?" Instead of answering, Simone nodded eagerly. "A curse cast for retribution. A curse that cursed the residents of Elmdale forever." Matthew began walking around the table while he spoke. "Who...why would someone do that?" She found herself asking. "For retribution. Man goes too far for vengeance. He is blinded by it and finally, it kills him." Matthew was peering up at the shadows now. "Shadows, are they also the outcome of the curse?" "No. We are the creatures of darkness, we called them to be our eyes and ears." He remarked, peering down at her from over his shoulder. An amusing smile was playing on his lips but his eyes were calculating, evil. Simone looked away.

"You are not Matthew Brown, are you?" Simone questioned, a large knot growing in her throat once again. "No, I'm not." "Then who are you, really?" She murmured, terrified to know the answer. With the way he grinned, her heart turned cold. "Someone you know very well." No, no, it couldn't be. "Show me your actual face." She implored him, closed her eyes, and hoped earnestly. When she opened them, she let out a sob. It was Nathan Woods.

CHAPTER 7

"Simone let out a scream",\s"HOW COULD YOU?" She shrieked at him and struggled at the chain keeping her to place. Nathan only cocked his head and watched her. Gone was the warmth from his face and his normal dimpled grin. How could this monster be her buddy for more than a month now? How could he be the one she had trusted and considered a friend? "YOU ARE LYING, YOU PATHETIC MONSTER!!" She shouted once more. The chain refused to liberate her. It only rattled against the iron bed.

"Simone, I care about you. If I hadn't, you wouldn't have been here." Nathan remarked kindly after she quieted down. She was breathing heavily and her arms ached. She didn't want to see his face. For a second, she believed she'd be able to recall who Nathan had been instead of the guy standing before her. "I will never harm you, feel assured." "What about the people I love? What about the residents of this town?" She growled, still refusing to look up at him. She heard him sigh before she felt the mattress compress beneath his weight beside her. She concealed her face behind her loose hair. "We are condemned to feed on the residents of this town." He replied gently yet his voice still sounded careless. With her heart sinking, Simone realized how it had always been like this but she hadn't noticed. "Without...without killing them, there is no way we would live." "Then die!!" Simon shot back with her clamped teeth. "That's what I'm intending to accomplish." At Nathan's words, she stilled. What was he talking about? "But I can't simply depart without bringing down Quinlynn and Juniper." He continued going. Now, Simone ventured to turn around and stare at him. He was peering unseeingly at something on the other wall. His hands indifferently grabbed a ball to and forth.

"How can I believe the words you are saying?" "Whether you like it or not, I'm still the same Nathan you've known for more than a month now." He answered calmly before he rose to depart. Simone closed her eyes, wrath scorching through every inch of her. Above her, the shadows shuddered and became calm once again.

Thwack! Someone smacked her cheek, hard. Startled, Simone gasped as she opened her eyes and saw Quinlynn kneeling over her. "Oh, there she is," Quinlynn remarked in a sing-song voice. When she stepped back, Simone gasped in disbelief. Vanessa was standing against the wall beside the entrance. The girl only grinned at her with her pointed teeth. Beside her, two females stood motionless. Their eyes were vacuous and their bodies dead. They seemed like they were in a fog. "What's....going what's on here?" Simone questioned, her eyes feverishly moving from one female to the other. Her heart was thudding and her veins humming. What was Quinlynn up to?

"I'm sure Trar'en fancies you, you know but before you daydream about being safe and everything, I wanted to show you something." Quinlynn giggled, strolling around Simone's bed. "What?" "You see, Trar'en hasn't eaten for a long time now. I'm sure he is short on his energy. Above you is the evidence enough." Quinlynn winked before glancing up. Following her gaze, Simone glanced up. The shadows were trembling. As Simone watched, one by one they dropped like rain droplets. Startled, Simone recoiled yet she didn't feel chilly. No darkness touched her. She dared to open her eyes at Quinlynn's joyful giggle. The shadows were nowhere to be seen.

"He is weak and he dares to rescue you. From me." Quinlynn remarked, leaning to level her face with Simone's. She was wearing bright red lipstick and thick make-up. She looked unnervingly lovely. Simone was terrified of her anyway. Terribly very frightened. "We've followed Trar'en for generations but today, we think that he is not capable of guiding us. I've stood with him all these time, I stuck by him even after he slaughtered two of ours in cold blood." Quinlynn really sounded a bit sad. When her long, red-painted nail touched Simone's temple, she shrunk back. With a grin, Quinlynn tucked loose strands of Simone's hair behind her ear. "I'm going show you something fantastic. Watch carefully." Quinlynn murmured. Before Simone could ask her anything, she heard footsteps outside the door, and then the door was forced open. She wasn't shocked to see Nathan there. His eyes were flashing brilliant ember, the sole clue that he was upset at Quinlynn's presence in the room.

"Oh hey lovely! We've been waiting for you." Quinlynn cooed as she sashayed towards him. Without lifting a finger, he sent her flying against the wall. Quinlynn managed to catch herself before she struck it. Vanessa confronted Nathan, to defend her pal. He made no move against her, however. When he shouldered past her, Simone understood why. He had made her immobilized. Shadows, darker than the normal ones were keeping her in place. Her arms were trapped to her sides. "I didn't realize you could become that pitiful!" Quinlynn remarked, sliding her tight skirt down and tossing her black hair over her shoulder. "I'm afraid I can't say the same of you. You've always been sad, irresponsible, and impatient." Nathan answered quietly, facing her with his hands in his jeans pockets. Quinlynn let out a mirthless chuckle. "But not foolish, sweetie." She remarked before she slammed one of the females against the wall exactly as Nathan had done with her minutes previously. Simone let out a moan in terror and concern as she heard a few bones break.

The impact was virtually instantaneous. Simone recognized with dread what Quinlynn was aiming for. Nathan sighed as he leaned down, his palms pressing on his temples. He gasped in agony which made Quinlynn cheer with satisfaction. "Come on, go ahead and feed. Show that little girlfriend of yours what you actually are." "Get...Get....lo...lost Quinlynn!!!" Nathan whimpered, sinking to his knees on the floor. "Oh darling, you can't do anything to make it feasible." She merely chirped in return. With a flick of her finger, Vanessa was free. "Stop resisting it, Trar'en. You can't deny who you are." Vanessa murmured, pulling the girl who had struck the wall by the back of her blouse. She shoved the girl in front of Nathan who jerked back as if hit by lightning. His face looked awful. It was pallid and he was shaking. "Oh come on! Stop spending the time battling what you desire most." Vanessa tutted. Quinlynn virtually forced the girl's face into his.

Simone watched the fight leave Nathan as he set his eyes on the girl. When he put his hands on the girl's temples, net-black veins erupted on every visible portion of his body. Simone gasped with dread when she observed blood being sucked from the girl's body. Nathan's eyes were closed yet he looked like a monster. What he genuinely was. Simone loved the darkness that appeared to overrun her consciousness. It was too much. She could not handle it.

She was trapped. No, someone was holding her. And running. She jerked open her eyes only to find herself gazing square at Nathan's face. The vision of him with black veins on his torso was unexpected. She shouted and he let her go in horror. Simone landed on the ground with a thud, jagged branches and stones pushed on her body, making her cry. "I'm sorry. You surprised me." Nathan was saying. When he reached out to lift her up, she batted his hands away. "Get away from me, you monster!!" "Simone, you need me right now." He answered hurriedly. Groaning, Simone attempted to stand up straight. Her legs failed her however, they gave out beneath her and she collapsed on the floor once again. When Nathan made no effort to get close to her, she let herself observe her surroundings. They were in the forest and the sun was sinking. With a terrible sensation, she knew that he was leading her to where he had gone the previous time. When he had been pretending to be hurt and had vanished in the mist. She looked at him with a clenched jaw. How could he play with her trust? Oh, he was a monster.

"Why did you bring me here? To murder me where no one can know?" She snarled. Rolling his eyes, Nathan sat down on a tree log. He squinted his eyes as he observed her. "As I said, I'm not going to hurt you. The only reason I've brought you here is that...help me remove this curse on the town." "How is that favorable for you?" Simone said plainly. An expression of hurt swept across Nathan's face almost before she could comprehend it being there. "It'll set me free." "Set you free as in you'd be free to walk the Earth and suck people of their blood?" A note of disdain colored Simone's tone. Nathan merely offered her a smirk. "No, free as in to murder us for once and for all." Simone's eyes widen. He was intending to murder himself and the other two. She opened her lips to protest that she did not trust him and that he was merely playing with her but got sidetracked.

Behind him, she saw shadows rising. They were darker and bigger than Simone had seen up till now. The wind moaned through the trees. Following her gaze, Nathan looked back and jumped up. He raced towards her and shook her shoulders to catch her attention. "Simone! Listen to me attentively." He said. "You are the only one that can make it happen. Destroy the dagger in the cave I led you to close once before. Destroy it and make us free." "Why?" Simone muttered, her body obviously quivering from the dread of incoming darkness. "Because I'm the creature of darkness which dreams of the light. And since I've begun to care."

He has spent years learning this specific trade. He wanted to revenge for the harm that had been done to him. "You have outlived your usefulness, my darling. It is time that you leave and go to where you actually belong." She had murmured in his ear. "I belong with you in the palace, your highness." He had remarked from where he was kneeling on the floor. "No, you do not. My father took you from the slumps and there you must return to." "Please, I implore thee. My lady, if I have done a crime, punish this servant of yours any way you feel necessary but do not send me back." He had appealed to her but she had only laughed at him. What had he not given her? Everything only to make sure that she sits on the throne which has been her rightful seat for eternity. He was a good soldier and had stayed by the princess all through. Was this how he was supposed to be repaid? Now that she got her lands back thanks to all the hard work he had put into his scheme, she was dismissing him.

The day had finally arrived. He sketched a pentagram on the ground, singing a wonderful song he had come up with himself. He sprinkled red stone dust on the border followed by spider's eyes in each triangle of the star and last, in the center he laid her knife. Her favorite dagger which her warriors were looking about in the countryside. After he was done, he waited. When the moon was far above in the sky and the wind moaned through the trees surrounding him, he began chanting. Soon, creatures emerged at each point of the star. Five entities donning the skin of human humans. He cackled at the sight of them. "Now, you shall feed on the people of this land forever." He clapped in excitement as the creatures stared at him. They were hauntingly beautiful. "Till when, sire?" One of them intoned. "Till this dagger is destroyed but rest assured, you cannot destroy it but only a human can. The one who will care for you despite knowing who you actually are. Someone who descends from the exact line of Margret Aurora Throckmorton, the lady who ripped it all from me. It shall never happen. You guys will see to that."

Nathan was tugging at her hand and she was trying not to trip over the fallen branches. The darkness was closing up behind them. She swore that she could hear Quinlynn's laughing carried across by the breeze. When they approached the area where she had come the previous time she had been in the jungle, Nathan halted. She was breathing hard but Nathan was great. As though he hadn't sprinted across the uneven woodland terrain. Just as Simone had feared, the mist began to build behind the bushes as they watched. "From here on, you have to travel alone.

That mist.....it burns us." Nathan remarked, letting go of her hand. Her heart was stammering in her chest and she bit inside of her cheek pretty hard. She wanted it to be a dream and wanted to wake up all perfect and normal. But it wasn't a dream for she tasted blood. "Simone, you need to hurry. I'll do my best to keep back the darkness but I can't guarantee you that I'd be able to do so for long." Nathan stated hurriedly. Taking a deep breath, she proceeded towards the cave entrance just beyond the bushes. The mist did not harm her. It was simply freezing. She paused. When she turned to glance over at Nathan from over her shoulder, she saw that he was already fending off the shadows with his own but he were feeble and no match for Quinlynn's and Vanessa's together.

"How can I trust you?" She yelled, conveying her anxiety. "Fine. Don't believe me but trust the Nathan you knew a month ago." He screamed back without even glancing at her. Clenching her hands into fists, she headed towards the cave entrance now hardly visible because of all the mist. Her trek to the door wasn't simple. Due to the mist, she could not see clearly where she was heading. Twice she stumbled but by pure luck managed to not get wounded. Soon she was walking inside the cave. It was silent. So quiet that she could hear her own uneven breath. It was dark too and she despised herself and Nathan for not thinking things through. The narrow passage started to widen as she kept walking. Somewhere, she could hear water trickling. Soon she could see an orange glow up ahead. She rushed towards it. The passageway opened up to a wide space. Rough rocks jagged out from the walls and floor of the cave alike. There was a fountain. A small one in the dead center. On that fountain was a dagger. Its hilt was brilliant crimson with blue diamonds. The orange light emerged from the water of the fountain. She could not see the source of it. As she carefully moved nearer the fountain, her heart began thumping faster. Her hands were moist and she could feel her shirt cling to her back.

"So, he's pretty busy." Simone jumped back in horror at Quinlynn's voice. She was standing in the shadows, wearing black and her arms folded over her chest. She had a nasty smirk on her face and her eyes were flashing amber. "Cat got your tongue?" She snarled. "What...how?" Simone staggered back a step. Nathan had informed her that it wasn't feasible for him to cross the mist. That it burns him but how did Quinlynn able to pass it? Unscathed at that. "He must've informed you that the mist burns him," Quinlynn murmured, effortlessly walking down to the floor. "He is feeble. Can't blame him." "What...do you want?" "You think I don't know what Trar'en is trying to do?" Quinlynn remarked loftily. "And he dares to imagine that he can succeed." Simone's heart wrenched horribly in her chest. She was going to die, she knew it. Quinlynn halted square in front of her,

her head inclined as she observed Simone. "Who is going to rescue you now, sweetheart?" Quinlynn lifted her hands as Simone attempted to walk away but her limbs failed her. She could not move. A cry froze in her throat as her gaze landed on Quinlynn's hands. Holes. There were gaping holes in the palm of her hands and from those holes, she could see needle-like......teeth. Quinlynn smirked mockingly. Simone closed her eyes.

Suddenly, Quinlynn screamed. Simone opened her eyes to see her flying away against the far wall of the cave. Surprised, she turned to see Nathan just at the entrance of the passageway. His skin was red and she could see several scars on his face. They were healing slowly. "I'm going to save her, Quinlynn. Don't you get ahead of yourself?" "Where....is Juniper?" Quinlynn growled as she stood up on her feet. Simone could see blood trickling down from the left temple. "Oh, Juniper?" Nathan mocked. Behind him, shadows formed. They were lighter than before. Nathan was running out of his strength. "Here she comes." He lifted his hand behind him and curled his fingers into a fist.

Around him, the shadows moved. Within a flash of an eye, there was something at his feet. No, it was someone. Vanessa. Burned black.

"NOOOOOO!!!!" Quinlynn wailed. "HOW COULD YOU?" "We've lived long and eaten on enough humans. It's time that we cease." Nathan said, stepping over what remained of Vanessa's body. Shaking, Simone retched. "WHY DO YOU CARE? YOU TRAITOR!!" With these comments, Quinlynn lunged toward Nathan and shoved him back with such power that he flew and smacked the wall behind him. Simone attempted to conceal herself behind one of the rocks. Her effort created a sound that drew Quinlynn. In a second, she was holding Simone up by the collar of her blouse. Simone strained to breathe. "It's all because of you, you foolish girl," Quinlynn murmured through gritted teeth. Her eyes were burning. "Let her go, Quinlynn. This is between you and me." "Is it?" She inquired, shoving Simone into the rock she was attempting to hide behind. On the touch, Simone's air whooshed out of her lungs and she fainted. It stung. She felt as though her backbone had been smashed into bits.

"SIMONE!! GET UP!!" Somewhere, Nathan was yelling at her. "GET UP!!" But Simone could not.

CHAPTER 8

"Simone, Simone wake up!!" Someone was stroking her cheek. She grumbled before forcing her eyes to open. She was still in the cave, resting down on the rough cave floor with her head on Jenna's lap. Jenna? What was she doing here? Simone sat bolt upright. "Jenna." She rasped. Her throat was dry. "Hurry, do something." Her companion begged with her and then glanced at something behind them. Simone followed her eyes. Nathan. He was terribly injured and he could hardly stand up. Quinlynn was unhurt. As the females watched, she turned on her heel and delivered Nathan a kick which sent him crashing against the wall. Then, he did not get up.

"You've stolen everything away from me. Juniper, Jordan, and Sebastian. You murdered them." She was saying as she hauled Nathan up from the ground by the collar of his shirt. He attempted to peel her hand off himself but he was too weak. With Jenna's support, Simone rose and glanced about to find anything,

anything to help Nathan. The dagger. It is still set in the middle of the fountain. She had to eliminate it. She moved her head towards it, quietly directing Jenna where to go.

"I don't know what you see in these pitiful human beings or why you even care." Quinlynn was hissing at Nathan who had his eyes closed. He was in a lot of agonies and instinctively Simone felt terrible for him. With Jenna's support, she ran towards the dagger. Their action allowed Quinlynn to throw Nathan flying against the opposite wall while within a blink of an eye she was right in front of Jenna. "And what do you think you are doing?" "Stop it, Brianna," Jenna replied, carefully moving back from her. "Stop what? Did you truly believe I would never find out about you?" "Well, you didn't. Not much which is why I'm here with most of my memories intact. At least the ones that matter." With these comments, Jenna shoved Quinlynn and went towards Simone. Bracing herself, Simone walked into the water of the fountain. It was chilly but not cold enough to numb her body. Still, she felt pinpricks on her skin which was in the water. She gasped owing to agony.

Behind her, she heard Jenna scream. "NO!!!" Simone yelled as she turned her head to see her pal. Quinlynn had Jenna up in the air from her hair. Jenna was weeping as Quinlynn laughed maliciously. "You're as pitiful as the rest of your sort. Think you are the best?" "Quinlynn!!! LET HER GO!!!" Simone yelled, squeezing her fists. It made Quinlynn laugh even harder but she did let Jenna go. Simone's companion fell with a bang on the floor and yelled owing to the agony produced by pebbles crushing against her body.

"You think you can win? Do you even know how to destroy the dagger?" Quinlynn intoned as she went around the fountain. She could not walk into it, Simone understood. "Nathan did provide me the summary of the curse. Only someone who loves about you may ruin it." "And you believe you are the one? Who cares about us?" Quinlynn questioned, reaching down to pick up a pointy rock. She could not walk into the fountain but she could toss something. With perfect precision, she could even murder Simone without touching her. Without giving her any reply, Simone rushed for the dagger just before Quinlynn targeted the stone where she had been standing. Her feet were numb. They could not move quickly enough. No, it wasn't only her feet. The numbness was spreading up her legs. Simone gave it everything she had as she extended her hand to take up the dagger. Just before Quinlynn was going to target her again, Nathan launched himself at her. Quinlynn let out a horrible wail.

"SIMONE HURRY!!" Nathan yelled. As soon as she touched the dagger, everything stilled around her. It was as though the time had stopped itself. Quinlynn was poised to hit Nathan but she appeared little more than a shadow. Nathan was preparing to put his arms over his face and Jenna was attempting to sit up.

As Simone stared, shadows emerged from the bottom of the cave. One of them was bigger and more ominous than the others. Its eyes blazed crimson. Terror stabbed in Simone's heart like a hot poker. "Is it you who desire to eliminate an old curse on this land?" Her shadow boomed. Simone swallowed violently, unable to look away from its gaze. Around her, everything was simply black. She could not see Jenna or the other two. "Yes." She croaked out the word. "Why?" The shadow inquired. Why? Simone mulled on the issue. Wasn't it because Nathan had very much commanded her to do it? No, it wasn't merely that. She wanted to defend the inhabitants of Elmdale from the monsters that had been feasting on them for ages. But that wasn't the full reason. She recognized that she cared about Nathan. She did want to assist him. Simone gazed up at the shadow, precisely mirroring his gaze. "Because I care." She whispered. "Dip the blade into the water of this fountain and utter these words. Chanomai daimonas, adetos tous. " "Greek," Simone murmured. "Who are you?"

"We are the shadows confined to this blade. For millennia we've witnessed the devils produce our family for their selfish purposes directly from this spring." The shadow answered. His grief was clear from his tone. "How?" Simone was confused. "By throwing in the people they fed on as sacrifices."

With these remarks, the shadows were gone. Dagger felt warm in her hands and things began moving again.

When Simone turned to check what was occurring behind her, she gasped. Nathan was hiding on the floor, shadows shooting out from around him. Simone saw mist too. It must be scorching him, she realized. After assuring that Nathan was as good as dead, Quinlynn moved for Jenna. She had not seen what Simone was up to yet. Her back was towards Simone.

Simone stared at Nathan once more. His eyes were begging for her to hurry. Mouthing 'goodbye', Simone plunged the blade into the sea. She heard a hissing sound as though it had been burning hot. Then she recited the words. The impact was instantaneous. Quinlynn shouted and hurried towards the fountain but she fainted halfway. She was withering in anguish and clawing at her face around them, the shadows were shouting. Only then did

Simone venture to walk out from the fountain. Jenna was staring about madly, her face pale and eyes wide. Simone hurried to her buddy and helped her up. Slowly, Quinlynn's body started to crumble. Jenna grabbed at Simone's sleeve. "What?" "Look." She pointed towards the fountain.

The shadows were dissolving into it. A few steps away from the fountain, Nathan was unusually motionless. Simone raced to him. He was hardly breathing and his scorched flesh wasn't mending. Gingerly, Simone lifted his head onto her lap. "You've endured enough." She whispered to him. Strangely, a large lump grew in her throat. Beside her, Jenna was unnaturally silent. Slowly, all the orange illumination disappeared from the cave. The water was drying. Nathan's body began to dissolve as well. "Oh, God." Simone wailed quietly. "Thank....you,"
Nathan remarked, his voice barely above a whisper. He could scarcely open his eyes. In those, Simone recognized his appreciation for her. Slowly and painstakingly, he moved his hand to touch her face. "Live...Happily." Trying

not to weep, Simone nodded. "You are free." She muttered as Nathan's fingers fell and his eyes closed. Within seconds, his corpse disintegrated into ashes in her hands and was blown away towards the fountain. Her hands were empty.

Simone woke awakened to the sounds of birds singing and her brother hammering on her bedroom door. Throwing it open, she frowned. "Are you insane?" "You won't believe it," Jayden remarked, his eyes wide. "Believe what?" "This town is in turmoil. About all the folks who departed unexpectedly, everyone immediately remembered that they were killed. By whom, they don't know."

Simone swallowed and pushed Jayden out of the room. "This town is odd." She murmured before slamming the door tight in his face. She hurried to the window and flung it open. Birds were singing in the trees and squirrels went up into them. People were hurrying around, seeming bewildered or agitated. With her heart heavy, Simone closed the window. Her gaze focused on the camera that was laying on her table. She hadn't left it there.

"Hey." It was Nathan in the video. Simone fell down on her bed when she saw what he had left. "When you'll be seeing this, hopefully, I'd be far gone. I truly want to thank you for helping me out and helping everyone out in Elmdale. I've lived for millennia and I've done every awful thing you can think of. But everything is done and I can't alter it. Go to Quinlynn's residence. You'll discover a trapdoor in her dwelling. It leads to a hidden level in the basement. I wish that you'd discover some of the missing persons alive. I truly hope so. One other thing, thirty years ago there was this family Quinlynn killed. Only a six-year-old child was saved. Her name was Sophie Throckmorton. I had delivered her to the elderly guy you met outside the town. I'm sure you must've seen him. Anyway, connect the dots and live well. Thank you, my buddy." Nathan concluded with a wink. The camera turned black and Simone noticed that her cheeks were moist due to the crying. Outside, the clouds thundered in the sky. She leaped up in astonishment when her phone rang from the closet. It was her closest buddy Nina from her former school. It was functioning. There were telephone signals all across the town. Smiling, she got dressed. It was time to see Jenna and embark on a rescue mission.

Thank You For Reading

Ryan E. Hunter

www.ingramcontent.com/pod-product-compliance
Lightning Source LLC
Chambersburg PA
CBHW051424150726